to *Drive* the Hundred Miles

Alec J. Marsh

DUXXX PRINTS PRESS

Schenectady, New York

TAGS

Genre: Modern with Magic
Rating: Explicit
Trigger Warnings: transphobia
Relationship: customer/employee relationship, family, f/m, siblings
Character Features: in the closet, lesbian (background character), self-esteem issues, trans male, wiccan
Other Tags: bad parenting, break up, christmas, clitoral stimulation, coffee shop, coming out, emotional abuse, first date, first kiss, first time together, flirting, fraught family dynamics, gaslighting, getting back together, magic realism, pov first person, past tense, reunion, smoking (casual), vaginal fingering, washington, winter solstice

Front cover by Pallas Perilous.
Edited by Nina Waters.

Published by Duck Prints Press, LLC. Schenectady, New York. Find our other publications and learn more about us at https://duckprintspress.com.

ISBN (ePub Edition): 978-1-946472-57-1
ISBN (PDF Edition): 978-1-946472-56-4
ISBN (Print Edition): 978-1-946472-98-4

This book was written on the unceded and unlawfully occupied land of the Duwamish people, who persist despite this theft. Learn more at native-land.ca

Chapter One

I WAS IN a tiny vintage shop in Nob Hill when Mom called me for the third time that day. I cast a furtive look at the attendant, who was helping another Christmas shopper, and guiltily answered the call. I didn't like to talk on the phone in public, but everyone else was busy and loud too, and if I didn't answer soon she would probably panic.

"Hi Mom," I said. I poked through a tray of tarnished silver jewelry. I didn't know what I was looking for, but it probably wasn't this. Mom had enough jewelry to put Stevie Nicks to shame. Hers was the last gift I had to buy, and the hardest.

"Oh, sweetheart, I'm so glad you picked up. I was getting worried." There it was. The invention of the cell phone should have been a boon to anxious parents, but sometimes I thought it was more of a leash because my mom expected me to be available at all times.

"I was at work." My voice came out more clipped than I wanted, almost sullen. It was hard for me to keep my tone even when she fussed at me.

"I called you six hours ago—"

"It was three," I said, and sighed. Temping wasn't a regular job, but it kept my hours roughly in the range of a 9–5, and Mom didn't seem to understand that. Whenever she talked about "adult jobs," she conjured up images of The Office, places where people sat around talking about their relationships and never actually worked.

"Look," I said, trying to steer the conversation back on track, "what was it you wanted to talk to me about?"

"I thought you were driving up today, and I wanted to know when you'd get in."

I carefully unclenched my jaw and took a deep breath before I answered. "I'm coming on Monday." I lingered on a pendant shaped like a pair of antlers that might have been ivory. It was pretty, but I wasn't shopping for me, and wearing jewelry increased my chances of getting misgendered. I moved on to a hat rack crammed with scarves in a riot of colors.

"The Solstice is Tuesday," she said. "That's barely any time at all. And I was going to cook dinner for you and Rhiannon tonight."

"I have to work through Sunday," I said. "Pre-Christmas rush." Answering angry tweets about toy availability wasn't my ideal weekend, but it was a good excuse to get out of spending more time with my family. As it was, I would be arriving the night before the Winter Solstice and leaving on Boxing Day, and those six days were about as much as I could stand.

"Aunt Hazel is coming over tonight, and she was so looking forward to seeing you."

I knew what to say in response. *Mom, please don't make me feel guilty for having other commitments.* I bit my tongue. It was a lot easier when I was practicing with a therapist, but I knew in reality that setting boundaries with her only made her defensive or teary, and it didn't actually change her behavior.

Passivity wasn't exactly the same as emotional maturity, but it was progress of some kind.

"I'm sorry," I said. "I'll see you Monday night."

"I swear you said you were coming this weekend."

That wasn't my problem. Mom always made me feel crazy, as if I was secretly terrible at communicating, as if I never expressed myself. When I had shaved my head and come out the summer before I ran away to Portland for college, she had cried about how she was so shocked and confused and wished I had told her sooner.

It wasn't my fault that none of my diatribes about gendered expectations had tipped her off.

"I wanted to talk to you about the Solstice ritual," she said. "I guess we should do it now."

I braced myself and grunted an affirmative.

"Were you planning on participating?"

"Why else would I come back that far before Christmas?" I blurted before I could stop myself. I tugged a brown cashmere scarf printed with orange autumn leaves out of the rack, and a dozen more came with it. I sorted through them, hanging them back up as Mom talked.

"Well, it's just...now that you're exploring other options, I wasn't sure you would want to."

I clenched my fists around the scarf I had been attempting to free. She was trying her best to be supportive. I knew this was her way of saying that I didn't have to participate. My family's coven was very into the divine feminine, and all their rituals were about invoking the Triple Goddess, thanking Mother Earth, bleeding onto the ground, the whole shebang. There had been no boys born to the coven in the eighty years since it was founded. No one except me, and it had taken seventeen years for me to figure out that cosmic mix-up.

Maybe I wasn't exactly dialed into the divine feminine. Maybe weekly rituals praising the moon cycle made me want peel my skin off, but I still resented that they had been taken from me. I had been raised to mark the wheel of the year with my family, and I felt adrift without those rituals.

"I want to be there," I said, and I meant it, and I regretted it. Someone would say something stupid and remind me that I didn't belong anymore. Either I was a woman and could do magic, or I was a man and was barred from it. I hated the dichotomy of their views, and I refused to let them shut me out entirely. I had never felt magic like they did, which I suspected was because I had been a man since long before I could put words to the feelings of emptiness I experienced. They didn't need to know that. They didn't get to feel superior because by accident of birth they were blessed with a gender identity that was deemed more sacred. I would be there in their circle, and they would be reminded that their sacred dichotomy wasn't as simple as they wanted to believe.

"Okay honey," Mom said, doubt clear in her voice. "I'm looking forward to seeing you."

"I'll text you when I'm leaving," I promised. The scarf I was currently twisting into knots was exactly her colors. I hoped she would like it.

I FOLLOWED THE familiar six-hour route north into the Wenatchee Forest, then through the increasingly narrow highways until I reached Serendipity, Washington. It was an old mining town, but the name had certainly been attractive to my great-grandmother, the founder of our coven. I felt a twinge of nostalgia as I drove between the old saloon storefronts mixed in with fast-food joints and boarded-up buildings. The sky was an icy blue bowl stretching overhead, ringed on all sides with mountains. It was beautiful in a way the city could never be.

Mom lived on the edge of town, practically urban. Most of the population lived in houses scattered along the single forest road that ran through town, surrounded by more lodge-pole pines than people. I parked in the driveway and took a moment to prepare myself. It was bitingly cold, and remnants of snow banked up over her carefully tended garden, but the walkway was clear.

The house looked the same as always, sage green, the roof sagging in the middle. It wasn't run-down, but there was an air of tiredness about it that showed how many people had lived in it. I looked at the silver moon painted on the door and steeled myself.

I pulled my backpack and duffel bag out of the back seat and headed up the steps. The porch was cluttered with weathered dining chairs, and pitchforks and snow shovels leaned haphazardly against the railing. I hesitated at the door, wondering if I had been away long enough to need to knock. I erred on the side of politeness and did.

It was the wrong choice, and I knew as soon as I did it. No one else in my family ever knocked, and they rarely called ahead to say they were coming. A love for rules was a unique trait to me, a desperate need for order in a chaotic world. It was the kind of gesture I saw as proper etiquette and everyone else saw as icy aloofness or pretension.

Mom opened the door looking worried and frazzled. Her eyes flicked over me, and for a moment I had the wild fear that she wouldn't recognize me. We hadn't seen each other since she'd driven down to Portland State to watch me graduate six months before, and I had changed a lot since then. Then I remembered FaceTime calls, and also, even if I passed now, I still had the same face as I'd always had.

I mirrored my mom in more ways than I liked: the same high-bridged nose (elegant, she had always called it), pale-blue eyes and brown hair that refused to have any semblance of texture. Mine was cropped short now, the sides shaved clean and smooth, and Mom's was streaked with gray, but we still looked related.

"Oh Goddess," she said breathlessly, and pulled me into the house. "Oh, sweetheart, oh—" She seemed at a loss for words. She traced her hands over my cheekbones, stronger since the T really started to take, and then over the stubble across my jaws. It still couldn't be considered a full beard, but just the shadow made me feel better.

"Will, are you hungry?" my sister Rhiannon interrupted Mom.

"Yes, please. Where's Misty?" My niece was three and would be a perfect buffer between me and the rest of my family.

"Brian has her for the night."

Distracted by Rhiannon's mention of food, Mom pulled away from me and hurried to the kitchen. My shoulders eased in relief.

Rhiannon pulled me into a tight hug. "You look great," she said. "I think your voice has changed more."

I wasn't sure I wanted the frank comments on my body any more than I wanted Mom's clumsy avoidance. It was still a relief to know that she wasn't going to be weird about it. Not that she'd ever been weird about that specifically.

"You look good too," I said, and meant it. Somehow, even with a toddler, she managed to look stylish and effortlessly feminine in the way I knew took a lot of effort. "How're…things?" I asked lamely. I glanced after Mom.

"She's thrilled to see you," Rhiannon assured me.

"I know," I said glumly.

"Will, don't," Rhiannon said in the long-suffering tone of an older sister. "Please, can we just get along for the week? You know how hard she tries, and she's been great about pronouns and everything lately."

I nodded, wishing I could avoid the song-and-dance of forgiving slip-ups that they'd had five years to correct.

Mom leaned her head back into the living room. "Come on," she said. "Pie's ready."

Chapter Two

MY BODY NO longer considered my childhood bed to be home, and I was awake just after six. I lay on the saggy mattress and tried to will my limbs to relax, but it didn't work. I had an entire day to spend with my family, and then the Solstice rituals at dusk and tomorrow at dawn, and anything could go wrong.

Eventually, I gave up and crept down to the kitchen, which was blissfully still quiet. The fridge was its usual mess of greens, weird health drinks, and jars of fermented vegetables. I boiled a few farm-fresh eggs and ate them on rye toast. There was no caffeine anywhere in the house—Mom claimed it blocked her chakras, but it was really because, even though she loved it, coffee was bad for her arthritis.

She came into the room, and my heart sped up.

"Good morning," I said, dumping my dishes in the sink. "I was about to get some coffee in town. Do you want anything?"

She hesitated. "No, I shouldn't."

I wasn't going to try to talk her into a bad habit. "Okay. Text me if you change your mind."

MAIN STREET WAS only a ten-minute walk, and I took my time. Most of the buildings remained the same, but the laundromat had a new, optimistic sign, and the drive-in burger joint had closed, probably squeezed out by the Jack in the Box down where Main Street met the highway. Next to the antique shop with a sagging roof was a new café, cheerfully labeled The Three Pines by the sandwich board in the parking lot, which had four spots. There was no sign on the building front, and it looked like half a house, with the other half a brewery. I studied both for a minute in confusion. They were trendy and extremely clean. They wouldn't have been out of place in Portland.

I was thrilled.

Inside was exactly the kind of bougie hipster coffee shop I haunted. The counters were dark wood polished to a shine, the tables small and uniform. Two armchairs sat in the window, a perfect spot for reading or watching the mountains.

I stepped up to the counter and scanned the menu. Besides espresso drinks, it offered frappes and chai lattes and Italian sodas.

"Hi! How can I help you?" the girl behind the counter asked. She was extremely cute in a cheerleader sort of way, her blonde hair done up in a ponytail and sparkles on her eyelids. She wore a baggy pink sweater under her brown apron. She looked…vaguely familiar.

"Do you roast your own beans?" I asked, then winced. "Sorry, wow, that sounded even more pretentious than it did in my head."

She giggled in a way that was obviously meant to soothe my embarrassment. It almost worked; she was that cute.

"We get them from a roaster in Seattle," she said. "We're not big enough to do it ourselves."

"That makes sense," I said. "Sorry for being a snob. I'll just have an Americano." I would try the local coffee beans anyway and see if they held up to Stumptown's warm richness.

"Sure thing," she said, and turned to the espresso machine. I leaned against the counter to wait until she was done so I could pay. I was pretty sure I'd gone to high school with her. She had been one of the girls who had ruled the school—not in a "teen movie" way, but because everyone genuinely liked them. Cheer squad, student council, school play—they'd been involved in everything. And I, an insecure egg who had avoided any trapping of femininity, had never bothered to learn how to tell them apart.

I was the asshole here.

"It's Will, right?" she asked as she poured my drink into a ceramic mug.

"Um, yeah. How did you know?"

She smiled. "I'm friends with you on Facebook."

"Oh." I blinked in surprise. "I, um, I don't know the last thing I posted on there."

She looked a little sheepish. "You coming out made kind of a big impression, so I remember you. I know you probably want to leave this whole town behind, but…anyway. And I'm friends with Selene."

"Oh. Um. Um, it's Bea, right?" I asked, relieved that I had remembered her name before I looked like an irredeemable tool.

"Yeah, that's me," she smiled brightly. "Sorry to, like, remind you that people gossip. I'm sure you don't want to know."

"I'm not surprised they talk," I said glumly. "I tried to stay away to give them time to adjust, but it's kind of inevitable."

"Everyone's got their own problems to distract them," she said. "Selene's been good about it, arguing with people on your behalf."

"Oh," I said for what felt like the millionth time. It really would have been nice if I could think of anything original to say. "I think Selene just likes to argue."

She laughed, then handed me my coffee.

"How much is it?" I asked.

"On the house," she said. "We'll see if these beans are up to your standards."

I grimaced, then dug through my wallet for change to tip her. "I'm sure they're great," I mumbled.

"Hey," she said, "It's not *my* coffee shop. I just work here."

"Actually," I said, "shouldn't you be off at college or something?" My cousin Selene was a senior at UW, so Bea must be the same age.

"Oh." Her face fell, and I felt like an asshole. Again. Then she had that sunny smile back on her face, a transformation too quick to be entirely genuine. "It wasn't really in the cards for me. But I've got a garden that's going really well, and an Esty store where I sell soap, and really, small-town life suits me."

"That sounds...peaceful," I said honestly. A quiet life in the country, some chickens, some soap. An ideal life if it weren't for the lack of community.

"Except for chasing rabbits out of the sage, it's not too bad."

She got the first genuine laugh out of me all week. "But you get to see rabbits."

"Very true. Thank you for showing me the bright side. How's your coffee?"

I had forgotten to even try it. I took a hasty sip; it was mostly hot. "Not bad," I said. "Not sure it's good enough to tempt me to move back, but not bad."

"A ringing endorsement from the city slicker," she teased.

Another customer came in, interrupting us, and I took my coffee over to the window seat with a feeling of regret.

Chapter Three

WE GATHERED FOR Solstice at Grandma's house. Her place was the center of all the family events, an aging, dark Victorian that was 15 minutes outside of town, pressed up against the edge of the woods.

I remembered from childhood a gathering of at least a dozen family members, aunts and great-aunts and cousins. This year was much smaller, but I had avoided coming back for the last few Solstices and didn't know if this was normal now. Cousins had grown up and left town for other jobs, and both my great-aunts had died in the last five years. That left my grandmother, my mom and her sister Allegra, her cousin Hazel, and Rhiannon as the only active members of the coven.

Allegra's daughter Ariadne had come home for the holiday, but that still made only seven of us gathered in Grandma's living room. She served up lunch—dry pot roast and tough kale salad—and I sat quietly while everyone else talked through their year. Ariadne was in the last year of her naturopathic degree and engaged to an environmental lawyer, and as the most accomplished grandkid, she took all the focus off of me.

I pushed pot roast around my plate and tried not to think about the ritual. I knew the rules, and I knew that I wouldn't feel the magic. I was okay with that. But if that became known to the women in my family, they would think they were better than me—for being women, for being cis. It wasn't something I could bear to talk about.

Ariadne and Rhiannon went into the kitchen to wash the dishes after dinner, and Mom and Allegra went upstairs to gather all the candles and other supplies. I hovered, knowing I should look like I was helping with the dishes but also knowing that I would actually be in the way.

Hazel tapped on my elbow. "Come outside with me?" she asked.

I nodded and followed her out to the covered porch. She sat on a bench that creaked alarmingly under her weight and pulled out her cigarettes, then patted the seat beside her. I sat on the arm, which leaned inwards but held. It was twilight already, the light dimming but not yet gone, and the sun hung low and clear in the sky. It was a perfect night for a sunset ritual.

I had always liked Aunt Hazel. She had done what I had done—come out and run away to the big city for a few years, though by the time I was born she'd become a fixture in Serendipity again. She was a terrible dresser, stomping around in her rain boots and house dresses no matter the time of year, and she chain-smoked and raised sheepdogs. She loved country living, and being a woman who loved women was something much easier for our family to accept than being someone who voluntarily became a man.

She held her Pall Malls out to me. "Want one?"

I shook my head. "Better not pick up the habit."

She nodded and lit up. "How's the job search going?" she asked.

I grimaced, but I could be honest with her. "Not great, but the toy company pays the bills."

"Nothing steady?"

"I did a bunch of interviews through this fall, but then the holidays happened and I slowed down." I'd been at the same office for a few months now, and it was shocking how easy it was to slip into complacency. My job was more customer service than advertising, and it was technically through a temp agency, but they showed no signs of cutting me adrift.

She nodded. "I expect there's a lot of competition in Portland."

"Yeah."

"I hurt my knee last year," she said, "and I can't keep up with the dogs anymore."

"I heard," I said. "You're still recovering?"

She laughed. "At my age, you don't ever fully recover from injuries. You just manage them."

"I'm sorry."

She shrugged. "I'm at peace with it, but I am slowing down. I could really use someone else in the house to do some of the lifting and carrying."

"There's no shortage of broke high-school students in this town," I pointed out.

"I'd rather it be you."

I blinked. That was exactly what she had been hinting at, and I had missed it. It was so unexpected, I had to sit and digest for a minute.

"Me?" I asked lamely.

"You know the house and the dogs, and I trust you. I know it's not your first choice of work, but I would rather my life savings go to you than someone I barely know."

As if there was anyone in this town who was fully a stranger. I reeled. My lease, my Oregon health insurance, my career...

On the other hand, this was my family. I loved Hazel, and if she needed help, it should be one of us taking care of her. I was sure she couldn't pay me much, but I wouldn't have to pay rent if I was living with her. I could slow down a little. College had been an exhausting grind of late nights and service jobs, and as much as I loved my studio apartment, I was tired.

I had friends in Portland, a plan, a future. Could I give that up? I liked Hazel, but could I live so close to Mom, to reminders of who I was in high school?

"I signed a lease through next July," I said.

"You don't need to move back immediately," she said. "I'm not going to keel over dead anytime soon. But I'd like you to think about it."

I nodded, and then the rest of the family came out and spared me the need to think any further about it.

WE HIKED OUT into a clearing in the woods behind the house. There wasn't a clear line where woods began; instead, there were two out-buildings among fruit trees, and then the pines slowly grew denser until they became ancient National Forest land. We didn't go deep enough to lose the meager daylight, instead gathering just inside the tree line.

Despite my family's reverence for nature, the clearing had obviously been created by human hands. It was almost perfectly circular, with small ground-level stumps where saplings had been trimmed down to maintain the space. Cobblestones marked out a pentacle in the dust, kept flat and barren by many sets of feet. The moss stayed among the trees.

The five members of the coven took their places at the five points of the pentacle and lit colored candles. Ariadne and I took white candles and filled in the empty spaces between two points. I felt more like an outsider now that there were only the two of us. When all the cousins came out, it felt less noticeable that there were tiers to our involvement.

The light was rapidly dimming, and we were illuminated only by candles, glowing warm in the gloaming, pale faces bright above our dark clothes. Despite the wrongness—the way they looked at me like I had betrayed them—standing here in this circle of chanting, wailing witches, a part of me felt at home.

I had always loved the rituals of the circle, from the time I was old enough to hold my own candle, back when I still wore long hair and floral Easter dresses, before I was old enough to spend long hours poring over books wondering why descriptions of men filled me with a longing so intense it felt like anger.

Grandma began to evoke the Triple Goddess, and a surge of emotion welled up in me. It was familiar, and I wanted it. I wished there was something out there that I could love without a matching surge of bitterness.

"We ask you, Mother, to protect us here," Grandma called out. "We ask you, Maiden, to remind us of the beauty of life. And we ask you, Crone, to give us wisdom, and to make our house a home. Another year is drawing to a close, and we thank you for guiding us through another turning."

I didn't listen to the words of the ritual after that. They didn't really matter. It was about the heat of the candle, and the wind on my skin, and the rustle of the leaves behind us in the night. I closed my eyes and savored the sensations. It was just above freezing, and a cold wind was blowing. The woods were peaceful. Maybe I could move back here, spend more time in nature. I liked Hazel and her dogs. There were other gods I could follow. I could find my own way.

A cold wind made our candles flicker, and I looked up.

Something moved in the woods behind my grandmother, and my skin went hot and then cold. My candle flame flared up like I had dropped grease on it. I blinked away light spots, and by the time I could see in the half light again, whatever had been in the woods was gone. Grandma was still talking like she hadn't noticed anything.

Everyone around me murmured, "Blessed be," and I echoed them a moment too late. The ritual was over, and the candles were extinguished.

Hazel turned on a battery-powered lantern, and we walked back toward the house.

I SLEPT FITFULLY again, tossing and turning on the narrow mattress. When I fell asleep, I was back in the dark woods, but I was entirely alone. I held a single candle, but the dream lighting illuminated far into the distance.

Movement to my left caught my eye, and I turned to see a pale stag. He had an enormous rack of antlers that seemed to phase through the trees as he walked toward me. I stayed perfectly still until he reached me. We stood face-to-face for a moment, and then he leaned forward and blew out my candle.

Chapter Four

A COFFEE ADDICTION, it turned out, was a perfect excuse to get away from the house long enough to breathe. It was snowing, a light dusting of flakes that stuck in drifts along the sidewalk and iced the road. I arrived at The Three Pines early enough that only one other customer was there.

My heart leapt when I saw Bea behind the counter. Her hair was up in a messy bun, and she was reading a book. When I stepped up to the counter, she smiled warmly at me. Her eyeliner had sparkles in it.

"Glad to see our coffee didn't drive you away!"

"It was good," I said, "and so was the company."

"If it's my company you're after, you must not have enough friends."

"My mom lectured me on the health benefits of alkaline water this morning," I said. "So as charming as you are, I'm also trying to avoid more of that."

She giggled. "Is the environment too acidic for her or something?"

I groaned. "Don't ask, please. I don't want to stop drinking my acidic caffeine death potions."

She nodded and moved behind the espresso machine to start my drink. "Same thing?" she asked.

"Please." I watched her work as the machine whirred and

hissed steam.

"How's your morning going?" I asked. She huffed. "That bad?"

"I was fifteen minutes late because I had to dig my truck out this morning."

"Is the blue truck in the parking lot yours?" I asked. It didn't seem like her kind of vehicle, more rust than paint and probably forty years old, but there weren't a lot of used-car lots up here, so people took what they could get.

"My dad's," she said, "but he's not working, and I live too far away to walk to work."

"I'll say. Where did it snow so much that you had to dig your car out?" Serendipity was at a high elevation, but the Cascades were so steep that an extra mile made a big difference.

"30 minutes east," she said. "Not a lot of jobs in a three-house town."

I whistled. "Did you live there in high school too?"

"Yep. Hour on the bus each way."

"And you did cheer after school."

She pulled the shot and then looked at me seriously. "You actually remember me."

"I knew your name!" I protested, like I hadn't remembered it mostly out of luck. "And I recognized you, we just never talked."

She shrugged. "I always felt kind of forgettable. Too plain and too much of a doormat to make much of an impression."

We had gone to a small enough high school that everyone made some sort of impression, but telling her that wouldn't be much comfort. "Well, I noticed," I said. "And I thought you were too pretty to talk to."

She grimaced, but she blushed a little. "Now you're just flattering me."

"And if I am? I'm still not lying."

She passed me my coffee, and I handed her my credit card. I paid and tipped, and then said, "You don't seem very busy. How do you stay open?"

"It's Christmas break, so everyone's schedule is weird. We mostly get skiers and hikers in here during the outdoorsy season."

I nodded.

"What do you do for work?" she asked.

I grimaced. "I'm the social-media manager for Franklin's Toys." I picked up my coffee and gestured toward the armchairs. She came around the counter to follow me; apparently it was slow enough that she felt okay doing that.

"You don't look pleased about it."

"My degree is in marketing," I said. "That's how I got the job. Well, I got a position at a temp agency, and they got me the job. But instead of doing ad campaigns, I mostly answer angry tweets about defective products."

"Do you get a lot of those?"

"You would be surprised. Usually it's people who don't realize the toys don't come with batteries or who can't be bothered to read assembly instructions."

She laughed. "I'm not surprised. A degree in marketing, huh? That's not what I expected."

"Why not?"

She bit her lip. "I feel like only boring people go into marketing."

"You barely know me. I might be extremely boring."

"I'm a very good judge of character, and I don't think you are."

It was my turn to blush. "Wait 'til you see my weekly planner," I said. "I color code appointments."

She hummed. "How do you feel about Excel?"

"Love it," I said.

"Is that why you went into marketing? The organizing?"

"Not exactly," I said. I had a positive spin on marketing, but I also had personal, extremely boring reasons for picking it that I didn't usually like to mention. She was watching me intently, though, like she actually wanted to hear, and she didn't seem turned off by my comment about my planner. Maybe she thought I was joking.

I decided to be honest. "It's not nearly as manipulative as people think," I said. "If you're doing it right, it's just connecting people to things they need or want, and communicating with them in a way that appeals to them. The stability appealed to me. I can make a career out of it for as long as I want. I clock into work, and I clock out. I always know where my paycheck and my health insurance are coming from."

"That's hot," Bea said sincerely.

My face burned even though she was probably being sarcastic. "I know how to have fun," I mumbled. "I just don't feel the need to have fun at work."

"I'm serious," she said, and her cheeks were also tinged with pink. "You grew up here too; you can see why I might like the idea of stability. You're being practical and thinking about your future. That's…more than most of us get to do."

"You have a future," I said quickly. "You have that Etsy business, and—"

She laughed shortly. Bitterly. "Maybe," she said. "Anyway,

I'm a simple girl. I see a man in a suit with a big paycheck, and I go all 1950s on myself." Her smile was cheeky, her return to cheerfulness sudden and disorienting.

"I don't wear a suit," I said quickly. "I work in Portland."

"You could though," she said. "You, Don Draper, in your fancy suit and your office with a view. I could come bring you a cocktail on your lunch break, and we could make out on your desk."

I choked on my coffee. I wasn't used to being flirted with like this. Even if I was the picture of Jon Hamm masculinity, most people weren't this overt. It was so blatant I couldn't believe it was real, which was the only reason I felt comfortable continuing the joke.

"Are you my secretary or my wife in this situation?" I asked.

"Your pick," she said, and smiled wider. Her front teeth overlapped a little. "I just know I would look really cute in one of those little sweater sets."

I laughed. "You would look cute in anything," I said. "Let's say you're my secretary. That means you get an office with a view too."

"An incredible view, if I get to watch you walk around in a suit all day."

She was really committed to this, and I floundered for a response. I had only watched one episode of Mad Men—I knew I probably should've watched more, but I was always busy and the nice clothes weren't enough to carry me through the rampant misogyny.

"Well, my secretary position is open," I said. "I can't pay you, but I'm sure we can work something out."

"I'm very flexible," she said, wiggling her eyebrows and destroying any impression she'd given that she was taking this seriously.

A customer in expensive-looking ski gear walked in, and she jumped to her feet. "Gotta go," she said. "Don't give my position away."

Chapter Five

Wednesday, I woke up to a message from Bea on Facebook.

"I'm so sorry to ask, but could you do me a huge favor? I need to go grocery shopping but my dad has a doctor's appointment in the opposite direction so we can't carpool. Could you maybe take me to Monroe? Everyone else I can ask is working."

I could have suggested that she wait for her dad to get home, but I wanted to see her again, so I messaged her back and cheerfully left the house.

Bea's house had the same weathered look as most of the houses on the mountain, the roof overgrown with moss and the front yard banked with pine needles. "Thank you so much," she said as she got into my Prius. "I forgot to get cranberries when I went shopping on Sunday, and now Mom's acting like Christmas is ruined."

"Cranberry sauce is the most important part of Christmas dinner," I agreed. "Especially if your mom's cooking is anything like my grandma's." I very, very slowly pulled my car out of her driveway, which was tilted and iced over in the shady parts. My Prius slid, shuddered, and lurched onto the main, slightly more traveled, road.

"Is it bad?" Bea asked.

"Everything is sort of dry and overcooked."

She laughed. "No, Mom's a good cook. But she loves cranberries, and only homemade sauce will do."

We drove out of the trees into a clear patch of highway, and I sighed. The clouds were dark and green overhead, filled with snow or hail, and the patchy trees stood out sharp and black against them. A single beam of sunlight cracked through, gilding the edges of the storm break with gold.

"Nice view," I said.

"It's always a nice view."

"I miss it," I admitted. Portland's weather was more temperate, the rain a constant drizzle, and I didn't mind, but I liked mountain storms.

"Sometimes I meet hikers or skiers who came here from hundreds of miles away, and I remember that I live somewhere beautiful," she said. "Most of the time it's just cold."

"Part of me wishes I could move back," I admitted. It was beautiful, and wild. People here had a routine, and familiar paths to tread.

"Move back?" she said, a little too loud. "You got out. What would you come back for?"

"Cities are loud," I said. "And they move too fast. I thought you liked it here."

"Sure, I guess," she said, but she didn't sound enthusiastic. I wished I could take my eyes off the road to look at her. "My life is fine. I'm near my family, and I have my garden. But you have a whole life in Portland. What would you give that up for?"

I wouldn't. As much as I missed parts of rural life, I had trans friends and medical support and queer book shops and takeout any time of night, and Serendipity didn't have any of those things. But the view as we drove down the mountain was almost enough to make me forget all of that.

"Hazel asked me to move in with her," I said. "She's getting older and needs someone who can climb stairs and help with her dogs." I hesitated, then decided not to say that talking to Bea made the prospect more appealing. I wouldn't be moving back *for* her; I barely knew her. But it was important to be reminded that some of the people here were good.

Bea scoffed. "You have, like, twelve cousins who still live in town," she said. "Any one of them could take care of Hazel. Why you?"

"She and I have always gotten along," I said. "And she's the only one who didn't get weird when I came out. Mom and Grandma…well, you can guess."

"So you queers had to stick together." She said it casually, the word tripping off her tongue like she said it every day, like the word was home to her.

I nodded. "I know someone else could do it, but I feel…responsible." I wanted to do more for her. Despite everything I said about the appeal of a job in marketing, I was still slogging my way through temp jobs and drowning in applications. I could give it up. My options would be narrower, but there would be less doubt.

"I know what you mean," she said slowly. "My dad's…well, he's got my mom, and he's got his disability checks, but what happens if I leave? What if something happens, and I'm not here to drive to the pharmacy for them or fix the computer?"

"Is he sick?" I asked, all worry about myself erased as I realized how selfish I was being. I wasn't the only one with family problems, but she smiled so cheerfully and flirted so relentlessly that I was always thrown off-kilter before I could remember to ask about her. I wondered if she was diverting my attention on purpose. I had been so caught up in seeing her again that I had forgotten a doctor's appointment two days before Christmas wasn't something people scheduled voluntarily.

"He's in early retirement," she said, her voice a bit distant. "Construction isn't easy on the body."

"I'm sorry to hear that."

"It's okay," she said. "He was in a union, so we aren't destitute. But my parents can't really survive on one income."

I exhaled and gripped the steering wheel tighter. God. How were we supposed to live like this? No wonder she wanted me to stay out so bad. I was adrift, but I had options, and her world was suffocatingly narrow. Her interest in my job came into sharp relief, too—not her attraction to me, but her attraction to the job, to the idea of sitting at a desk and investing in a pension.

"It's good of you to take care of them," I said.

"There's nothing else I could have done," she replied grimly. "And like I said, it's not so bad."

"If it wasn't so bad, you would be happy I was thinking about moving back."

She made an odd choked sound, and I risked a glance at her. She was staring straight ahead, eyes bright. "Will…" she breathed.

"It's okay," I said. "You don't have to be happy about it all the time. I know what it feels like to be trapped."

"It's different for you," she said. "You had to come out, and I know how hard that must have been. I can stay in the closet my whole life, and it won't affect me."

Her confession felt so natural I barely lingered on it. "Hazel's out," I said. "You could come out."

"It's too much work," she said. "I'm not like you. And it's not like there are any girls I want to date anyway, so I don't want the hassle." She drew in a shaky breath. "But just once, I want to go to a Pride parade and not feel like I'm alone."

I took my right hand off the steering wheel and reached out for her. She squeezed it tight enough to press the bones together, and she drew another shaky breath. Despite the serious conversation, heat flowed through me at her touch. "Sorry," she said. "This isn't really important, in the big scheme."

"Come to Portland," I said quickly. "You can stay with me for as long as you want."

"My family is too important," she said.

"You don't have to move out," I said. "Just take a week off. I'll bring you to a dance club, and the queer coffee shop, and we can go clothes shopping."

She rubbed her eyes. "That sounds so nice. I want it. I really do."

"I'm sure your parents want it for you," I said. "I know you're not ready to move away, but it's something, isn't it?"

"It's something," she agreed.

Chapter Six

I WAS SUPPOSED to spend Christmas Eve with my family, but then Mom sent me to the store to buy sugar, and I took the opportunity to stop at The Three Pines again. When I stepped in, the brunette behind the counter gave me a knowing look and then yelled, "Bea, your suitor is here!"

She slipped out of the back and raised an eyebrow at me. "I wasn't expecting to see you today."

"You should have," I said. "I like to have a routine."

"The usual, then?"

"No," I said, quickly, "Why don't you surprise me?"

"Careful," she said. "If you try too many new things at once you might faint."

"I think I can handle it," I said.

"Better go sit down, just in case," she said with a smile. "I'm going to go on break in just a second, so I'll bring it to you."

She brought my drink in a ceramic mug I recognized because I owned the same Target set. Boring, but easily replaceable. When she gave it to me, our fingers brushed, and electricity danced between us. I pulled away and narrowly avoided spilling hot milk over my hand. To cover my clumsiness, I brought the mug close to my face and inhaled fragrant chai.

"Vanilla," I said. "Trying to cast a love spell on me?"

"I might be," she said. "Drink it, and we'll see if I'm a witch."

I laughed and took a hesitant sip. It was hot and earthy from the hemp milk, the vanilla and cinnamon mingling to create a flavor like a wintery dessert. I liked my chai spicier, but her blend matched her sweetness perfectly.

"I think your experiment will be flawed," I said. "Too many confounding variables."

"I didn't think the son of a witch would be concerned with the scientific method." She tucked herself into the chair opposite me.

"I needed to get some healthy rebellion in," I said. "And she's mostly just an old hippie who doesn't like going to the doctor."

"She told me she was a witch," Bea said with a note of petulance in her voice. I sighed. "Is it a secret? No one in your family acts like it is, and everyone's given up on clutching their pearls about it. She buried charm bags on either side of the main road last year when there were wildfires."

"It's not a secret," I said. "It's just embarrassing."

She laughed. "You're so serious, Will. If it makes them feel better, why be upset? Besides, if I could do a spell and protect myself, or bring myself prosperity, I would. You're lucky to have some sort of faith."

"I don't—"

"You know what goes in a love spell, don't you?"

I did. I knew everything I had been raised with, but I also knew everything I had researched myself, trying to expand my knowledge, trying to find something that made me feel powerful without invalidating my gender. That tiny moment during the Solstice made me want to try again.

"Yeah."

"I don't see the harm in letting them believe."

"It's not about belief, exactly. The spells work," I admitted, "for everyone else."

"Oh," she said.

I didn't want to get into it. I couldn't. Her big, welcoming eyes weren't enough to get me to pour out my hurt, not yet, although I could already tell she would wear me down.

"Will you do a spell for me?" she asked. "It can be a simple one."

"I don't know if it'll work," I hedged. "I don't seem to have the right juice."

She chewed on her lip. "It's because you're trans, isn't it?" she said bluntly.

"I…"

"Sorry," she said. "We don't have to talk about it."

"No," I said. "You're right. Since I've come out, all of it has felt…" I waved my hand. "There's baggage. But fuck that. Fuck the Moon Goddess. I'll show you what I can do."

A smile broke across her face, and I was momentarily stunned. She was always smiling, always giggling, but this smile met her eyes in a way that made my heart leap to my throat and stay there. I would do much stupider things to get more smiles like that from her. "I'm excited," she said. "I never felt comfortable asking your mom, but I trust you."

"I can't promise anything," I said.

"I know."

"When do you get off work?" I asked. "I'll meet you. I need to get some supplies."

❄

I PICKED HER up in my Prius right at 3 p.m. She probably knew I had been waiting nervously in the parking lot for 15 minutes—it was a very small parking lot, and I could see her closing up through the big picture window. She must have seen me. I didn't care. It showed that I was excited for our—whatever this was. It felt like a date, at least to me.

I resisted the urge to get out and open the door for her as she crossed the parking lot to me. It felt polite, but also like overperforming masculinity in a way I couldn't quite pull off. She opened the passenger door and let herself in. Her coat was a practical black raincoat, but she wore a powder-blue scarf with bright-pink paisley that matched her flushed cheeks. "Where are we going?" she asked.

"Out of town a little bit," I said. "We won't go all the way into the woods; we would have to walk back in the dark. But I want to get away from other people."

There was a brief, tense silence.

"Shit," I said. "We don't have to. I realize how creepy that sounds."

"No," she said. "I trust you."

"You shouldn't trust strange men just because they offer to show you magic."

She raised an eyebrow. "You aren't strange. You're…" She trailed off, then looked away. "You're safe."

Because I was trans? It was generally true. I'd had to opt-in to masculinity, and that meant that, hopefully, I had avoided the predatory parts of it. But the principal of the matter was that I couldn't ask girls on dates in weird places. Sometimes I forgot.

I couldn't say any of that. It would come out so fucking condescending that I wouldn't be able to stand myself. I was safe to trust, and she trusted me. That would have to be enough.

I started the car and drove out onto the highway until I

reached a wide enough pull-out. The river was high this time of year, and the rocks were slippery, but there was a little copse of trees between the shoulder and the cliff.

I laid a quilt on the ground and sat down.

Bea sat across from me, cross-legged.

"We won't be out here long," I promised. It was the warmest part of the day now, the temperature just above freezing, and the wind got funneled along the river where there weren't any trees to break its path. I started pulling supplies out of my backpack.

"What spell did you pick?" she asked.

"I thought I would start with a simple blessing jar," I said. "You put in things that call your intentions toward you, and then seal it and keep it by your bed until you get what you want."

"What will this one be?" she asked.

"It's for you," I said. "I thought a prosperity jar would be nice."

"Hell yeah," she said. "I could always use more money."

She said it lightly, but I knew what living in this town meant. I pulled out a flask of brandy and passed it to her. She sniffed it and then took a sip.

"That's just for us," I said. "Because it's cold."

"You know alcohol is bad for cold weather," she said.

"Yeah," I agreed, "but like I said, we won't be out here long." I arranged a circle of tealights around an empty mason jar.

"Tell me what you're doing," she prompted.

"I don't know why we put candles around everything," I said. "But they feel right. Like a...magnifying glass, I guess. They enhance a spell."

I poured in brown sugar. "To draw kindness and generosity to you."

I added dried vervain. "For prosperity."

I rolled a fresh spearmint leaf between my hands, and the sharp smell filled the air. "For luck and fortune."

I added a single new penny, gleaming bright, and let it speak for itself.

Then I pressed a green spell-candle into the pile of ingredients at the bottom of the jar.

I took a deep breath. I probably should have centered myself before we started, but I hadn't thought about it, and it was too late now.

"I'm going to light the candle," I said. "Then I'll call on the energy of the Earth to seal my intentions in. Once I start talking, don't interrupt, please."

"What will happen if I do?"

"I'll lose my train of thought," I said. "And it will be really embarrassing for both of us."

She nodded seriously.

I pulled a pack of cigarettes out of my basket. "Tobacco is for increased confidence and strength," I said. "It's a good element to add to any spell. I'll light it at the end of my prayer and pass it to you. You'll blow smoke into the jar right before I seal it."

She nodded. "Do you smoke?" she asked.

I flicked open the pack to show her twenty pristine cigarettes. "The way Catholics drink wine," I said. "Fresh is better, but this is what I had." They were a pack of Camels from the gas station; using Mom's stash of rolling tobacco would have meant admitting to her what I was doing with it, so I had skipped that part.

I pulled out a book of cheap matches and lit the candle.

"Earth below us," I said, "I call on you, support this woman. Water of the river, I call on you to bring fresh energy to us. Wind of the mountains, I call on you to take this woman's voice and carry it far and wide. Great fire, light up this woman's creativity, let her burn slow and hot, let her power warm those around her." Energy tingled across my skin. My chest was heavy, but I drew a deep breath, straining against the confines of my binder. My fingers ached from the cold, but I couldn't put on gloves. The candle flame danced in the jar, then flared up, bright and intense. I felt again the strange heat that surged through my skin. Bea inhaled sharply.

"Bless this woman and take her under your protection," I continued. I should have called on the Great Mother, but I couldn't do it. She wasn't for me anymore.

Something slid across my consciousness, deep and demanding. I looked up, into the thin stand of trees. A figure stood there, pale and undefined, crowned with antlers. He looked like he stood hundreds of feet away, as if I looked at him across a vast expanse, all his edges faded out. I had walked by those trees; he was maybe ten feet away. Any farther and he would be in the river. His antlers were magnificent, bone white and twenty-pointed, but when he stepped forward, they seemed to shiver and pass through the trees.

"Horned God," I named him. "I thank you for coming, for hearing my plea. I thank you for your notice. Bring blessings to Beatrice Danielson and increase her prosperity."

I blinked, and the figure was gone. He might have been nothing more than fog. Already he didn't feel real. I turned back to the jar, to the rules I understood. I held the cigarette to the candle flame and let it catch fire, then inhaled until the cherry caught. I passed it to Bea. She held the cigarette delicately, between thumb and forefinger, and inhaled.

"Do I say anything?" she whispered.

"You can thank the Earth," I whispered back, though the hushed tone wasn't necessary.

"Thank you, Horned God," she said, voice clear and confident. Then she put the cigarette back to her lips and exhaled into the jar I held out to her. I dropped the lid atop it, extinguishing the candle and trapping the smoke.

I didn't have anything left to say, so I broke the circle. "Thank you, spirits, for coming when I called. I return you to the woods."

The silence felt like air leaking out of the balloon, and I was suddenly empty.

Bea met my gaze, her lips slightly parted. Her eyes were wide and dark. The smell of the still-lit cigarette hung between us.

"Wow," she said softly.

I had done so many spells.

I had never before believed any of them had worked.

"Wow," I agreed. I leaned across the small space between us and pressed the warm jar into her gloved hands.

She took it with an air of reverence. "Thank you," she said. "How do I take care of it?"

"Put it by your bed," I said, "or under your bed, if you have to hide it. It should keep working on its own. If you want to charge it again, take it out and light the candle, say a blessing, and add more smoke. The blessing can just be one sentence, you don't need to do the whole..." I waved my hand vaguely. "Or don't," I added quickly. "It's just..."

I was suddenly embarrassed. The magic had felt different, but I felt different every time I touched her. Was it that I had done a spell, or that this could arguably be called a date? Was the energy I felt just her eyes on me, her interest? The figure in the trees could be nothing more than the memory of a dream, a wish.

"This was…" Bea stared at the jar in her hands, face oddly serious. "I felt it. Something. I don't know what I was expecting, but…"

I wanted to deny it, laugh it off. "I felt it too," I admitted instead.

"You're something special," she said.

"Me?" I protested. "I'm just doing what I was taught. You're the one who believed, who got me out here in the first place. You could have treated it like a joke, but instead you…" I couldn't think of how to express what I wanted to say. That I wanted to believe because she believed. That everything she did made me feel warm inside. That I loved the way she smiled and loved her seriousness more. That she didn't make hope or belief seem childish.

"We all need to believe in something," she said. "It may as well be this."

I DROVE HER back to her truck in the rapidly settling twilight. It was just past four and already sunset. I sat in the driver's seat trying to find something to say, some excuse to keep seeing her. I would have done just about anything, except invite her back to my house. She sat quietly, holding the spell jar pressed between her palms.

"Will you be safe driving in the dark?" I asked.

She laughed. "How old do you think I am?"

"I worry!" I said. "I can't help it."

"I drive home in the dark every day," she said. "Will you be safe driving this tin can on the ice?"

"I think I can handle a ten-block drive. Text me when you get home?"

She plucked my phone from the cup holder and swiped it open. She typed at it for a minute and put it back without letting me see it. "That was very smooth," she said.

It would have been a lot smoother if I had realized I didn't have her number already. It was just instinct to worry about those close to me, those who had long walks home or late-night buses to navigate or narrow, curvy, icy roads to steer up steep mountains.

"You know me, a regular Casanova," I said. "Hopefully without dying of syphilis in the third act."

"Didn't Casanova cheat on all his girlfriends?"

He didn't, but I didn't want to get into a history lesson. I shrugged. "I can be reformed."

"Mm," she said. "A project."

"I prefer a man who reforms himself to impress someone."

She looked at her lap. "I think I could put the effort in," she said, "for a man with a suit and a big paycheck."

I whistled. "That's my cue to leave. I don't want to get between you and your dream man."

"I should get home anyway," she said. "We do family dinners on Christmas Eve."

"Shit," I said. "I'm sorry for keeping you. Of course you should go."

She reached for the door handle. "I...had a really nice time today."

"Me too," I said. "I..." I couldn't ask to see her tomorrow. Tomorrow was Christmas. "I'm leaving on Boxing Day," I said.

"Maybe we could get breakfast together?"

"Won't your family want to see you off?"

"I'll lie to them," I said quickly. "Or I'll just say goodbye in the morning and then meet you after. They're getting me all day tomorrow."

She nodded. "I'd like that. I'll text you in the morning?"

I nodded, and the silence stretched out between us. I wasn't quite ready for the conversation to end. She opened the door and cold air swirled in.

"Drive safe," I said.

"Only because you told me to," she said. Then, she shut the car door sharply and twisted in her seat. "Are you going to offer to kiss me goodbye or not?"

I really, really shouldn't. I had one meeting with her left, and then I would be going back to Portland. No matter how much I liked her, no matter how much I liked the romantic idea of it, I knew I couldn't move back here. I had a life in Portland, one full of more possibilities than could be imagined here. And no matter how much I liked her, I couldn't ask her to move to Portland. She had her business here, and her garden, and her parents. If she wanted to leave, she already would have.

I waited too long, and she said, "Sorry, never mind," and got out of the car.

"Wait!" I cried and scrambled out my door. "Wait, sorry. Can I kiss you goodbye?"

Her cheeks were bright pink, but she said, "You better."

I hurried around the car and stopped in front of her. She still held her jar in her hands, but she put it on the roof of the car and stood, waiting for me. I thought, for a second, about bending her back in a dramatic, sweeping dip. She would probably think it was funny, but something told me this kiss was important. I had to take it as seriously as possible because I was going to remember it.

I stepped forward and slid a hand around the back of her neck, warm from her cashmere scarf. She watched me, lips parted, eyes wide with the same kind of seriousness that I felt. We were the same height, and it was nice to meet her as equals, to lean right into her.

I had always thought people were exaggerating when they talked about first kisses being special. I expected that finding "the one" would mean growing closer and closer to someone until I woke up and realized that I couldn't imagine my life without them. Whatever magic people talked about had always felt like a romantic embellishment.

Then my lips touched Bea's, and our mouths slid together, and something in me lit up. I had kissed so many people— friends late at night, strangers at bars, partners and first dates. None of those kisses had felt like this, warm and safe and still expansive. My world burst outward as electricity fizzed through me.

She slid her hands across the small of my back and pressed us closer together. My jacket hitched up, but I barely noticed the cold on my bare skin as I answered her nudge and pressed her against the car. As long as I was kissing her, I felt like I had all the time in the world.

She pulled away first.

I didn't want to stop.

Her lips parted, and her tongue darted out to moisten them. I leaned in again and sucked gently at her lower lip. Our next kiss was a little deeper, her mouth opening softly, my tongue sliding against hers, but it was still slow, gentle. She pressed her fingers into my back. I pressed a hand against her hip under the hem of her jacket. I couldn't get at bare skin without going under the hem of her dress, but I didn't feel too upset about that. I could get there next time.

That thought brought me back to the reality of kissing her, or rather back to the reality of how limited our time for kissing was.

She paused again, but she only pulled away a fraction of an inch. When she spoke, her breath tickled across my lips.

"What if we got back in your car?" she asked. "Your jacket is really getting in my way."

I exhaled. "I thought you had to get home."

It was too dark to get a good read on her expression, but the curve of her cheek was lit up by the yellow streetlamp.

"I do," she said. "But dinner won't start without me."

I should have argued.

I kissed her again instead.

Her phone went off, the vibrations pressed between our hips.

"Crap, sorry," she mumbled and went fishing for it. I leaned forward, pinning her against the car, and pressed my face against her warm throat. Her scarf smelled like a bakery.

I could hear whoever was on the other line. "Where the hell are you?" he asked. "Your mom's been cooking all day and you can't even be home for it?"

Bea tensed under me.

"I got stuck at work," she said. "Sorry, I had to mop—long story. I'm just about to leave."

"It's Christmas," he said. "You should have left early."

"I told you I'd be working," she said tersely. "I'll be home soon. Love you." She locked her phone and shoved it back in her pocket.

I stood up and backed away to give her a little space. "Sorry for monopolizing your time."

"It's not your fault," she huffed. "I told him I was working today. He's always worried about money and telling me to pick up extra shifts, and then when I do, he acts like it's a major inconvenience or complains that I took the truck."

"I'm still sorry," I said. "Do you…want an excuse not to go home?"

"No," she said, but she didn't sound sure. "My mom has been cooking all day, and I'm looking forward to it."

Neither of us moved.

"You'll have to let me out," she said.

I stepped back. She took several steps toward her car, then hesitated.

"See you Sunday?" I asked.

She nodded. "Merry Christmas, Will."

I GOT A text halfway through dinner. I pulled my phone out under the table. "Betty Draper" had texted me.

Betty Draper
Home safe and eating turkey. Looking forward to my winning lottery ticket.

I forced down a smile and replied.

Me
Glad to hear it. Don't divorce me when you're rich.

Chapter Seven

MY FAMILY MIGHT be pagan, but they were as susceptible as the rest of America was to the gods of Christian capitalism. It was unavoidable, and with small children around, there was a lot of motivation to conform. Three-year-olds didn't consider freezing in the woods to be an acceptable alternative to presents.

I didn't want to be alone with my thoughts at any point, especially not when preparing to see my family, so I made cinnamon buns. It was a complicated recipe that required me to knead the dough twice and rise it over a heated oven. I was good at it, and I could weigh my ingredients, line up my timers, and create a perfect breakfast every time. That the kitchen was exactly as I had left it five years before was more off-putting than comforting. Mom should have moved on by now, or rearranged, or gotten new appliances. Both her kids had flown the coop, and she was still here, walking the same paths and cooking the same meals. I hoped she felt happy, not trapped.

I washed the dishes while the dough rose for the first time, then I got the fire in the living room going. I had brought some black tea home that I liked, so I made a cup of that and listened to the house creak and the fire crackle. It felt like companionship. The solitude was comforting, familiar. In my apartment in Portland, there was always the sounds of other people, and I still felt achingly lonely.

I kneaded the dough gently, rolled it out, and sprinkled in the cinnamon. Then I rolled it up and tucked it into the pan

to rise a second time. I pulled out my phone and texted Bea a
picture.

Me
One hour to breakfast.

I got a prompt response.

Betty Draper
Be right over.

I replied earnestly. It was too early for clever banter.

Me
You're always welcome.
I wasn't expecting you to be awake.

Betty Draper
I had stuff to do. You, on the other hand, are evil. When
did you wake up?

Me
Cinnamon rolls don't bake themselves. I got up at 7.

Betty Draper
Evil.
Merry Christmas, by the way.

Me
Merry Christmas. Did Santa bring you anything nice?

Betty Draper
No, but he brought me something naughty.

I laughed out loud, muffling the noise with my hand in case
Mom was awake.

Me
Pics?

Betty Draper
You'll have to buy me dinner first.

Me
I think that can be arranged.

Betty Draper
I'll hold you to it.

MOM CAME DOWNSTAIRS then, and I hastily stuffed my phone in my pocket. I wasn't ready to explain to anyone why I was smiling like a moron. She swept into the room and somehow managed to make noise even though she wasn't wearing shoes or tinkling jewelry.

"Merry Christmas, hon!" she said cheerfully. "It smells amazing."

I shrugged. "I couldn't sleep."

She patted me on the shoulder as she forced her way into the kitchen. "Do you want tea?"

"I'm okay," I said. "I already made myself some."

"I'm going to make spearmint," she said. "That feels festive, right?"

I pressed myself into the back corner of the kitchen while she pulled out the teapot and kettle and several jars of dried herbs. "I picked the mint myself," she said. "There's a big patch up on Allegra's property, and it's better than grass, you know. It covers the whole hill, and we all went out and picked as much as we could, and it didn't make a difference. It's such a miraculous plant, very strong and masculine."

My shoulders climbed up around my ears. I hated the taste of spearmint.

"I'll send some home with you," she said. "All that coffee you drink isn't good for you."

There were a lot of things that weren't good for me, but

Mom didn't need to know about my diet or my daily habits. I would only be here for a few days, and I would avoid talking about all of that.

"Thanks," I said instead. I would take it home and leave it in my cupboard, and everyone would be happier than if I argued. "I should put the rolls in the oven."

She clattered around for another minute, let the kettle come to a whistling boil, then poured her herbal concoction and took it to the kitchen table. I set the oven timer and then swept the floor, just so I could have something to do with my hands.

Mom talked about her volunteer shifts at the food bank and complained about their bad management while I made the required noises of interest.

The cinnamon rolls finished baking, and I pulled out the ingredients to make icing.

"What are you doing?"

"I'm making cream cheese glaze?"

Mom's nose wrinkled. "You really should make a boiled icing. There's a recipe in the family box."

The family recipe box was old and stuffed with index cards; it was a treasured heirloom that I knew was fated for Rhiannon someday.

"I don't want to make boiled icing," I said. "And I bought the right ingredients for cream cheese glaze."

"That's not the traditional way to do it."

"I've made these a dozen times," I said, and there was that petulance in my voice that I hated so much.

Mom heard it too, because her voice wobbled when she replied, "I was just trying to help."

"I appreciate it," I said, "but I have a plan, and I want to stick with it."

"Fine," she said. "It's your choice. I'm going to feed the chickens." She closed the door a little too hard on the way out.

PEOPLE WERE SUPPOSED to arrive at ten, but ten came and went. I scrubbed down the counters, and at 10:45, when the house was still empty except for me and Mom, I mopped the floor.

"What are you doing?" she asked from the doorway to the kitchen.

I tugged my headphone out of my ear and muted my podcast. "What does it look like?" I asked.

"I cleaned before you came. This isn't necessary."

I bit back a sigh. "I spilled sugar on the floor," I said. "And I'm…trying to keep busy while I wait for people to show up."

"It's Christmas!" she said, sounding offended. "You could at least read a book or something."

Something normal, she meant. I would have loved to read a book, but I was filled with too much restless energy to sit still, and if I had to be alone with my thoughts, I would linger on bad memories.

"I don't mind," I said. "I made a mess baking, and I can clean it up."

She sniffed.

"Have you heard from Rhiannon?" I asked quickly. "She's later than I expected."

"She has a toddler," Mom said. "She'll get here when she gets here."

I raked my fingers through my hair. She was right, of course. And it wasn't like we had to be anywhere. The party didn't start until Misty got here, and all we planned to do was open presents and eat snacks. But we were supposed to have started at ten, and now my internal clock was thrown off, and my nerves were mounting.

To my relief, I heard the sounds of tires on gravel outside, breaking the tension between us.

IT WAS AUNT Hazel and Grandma, but Misty arrived only a minute later, damp and loud, her parents trailing behind.

"It's snowing!" she announced gleefully.

I hurried to the window and looked out. Sure enough, wide, fat flakes were floating gently out of the sky and landing on the frozen lawn.

"It's a blessing," Hazel said cheerfully.

"If only Selene could be here, everything would be perfect," Mom said.

Misty shrieked from the other room that there were presents, so we gathered up the food that Mom had made and moved into the living room to watch Misty open her gifts.

MOM LOVED THE presents I got her—or she had become a better actor than I remembered. She buried her face in the scarf and smiled. "It feels amazing, hon!" she said. "Thank you."

She passed me a small, wrapped package. It was thin enough I thought it might be a gift card, wrapped to make it feel special. Not that I would have minded—a gift was a gift and cash was cash. I slit the tape and undid the paper to see a small tan jewelry box. Inside was a flat moonstone pendant on a leather thong. I stared at it for what felt like minutes, trying to understand.

It was as pretty as moonstone always was, the striations of

blue and silver inside the creamy white body catching the light as my hands shook. The setting was simple silver, letting the stone shine. It was…

"It's for self-love," Mom said. "Moonstone is very healing."

It was an unambiguously feminine stone. Anything associated with the waxing and waning of the moon was. It might have been meant for self-love—Mom knew her crystals—but it was still a slap in the face.

I tried to imagine saying out loud that I didn't like my necklace because it was a girl rock, and I wanted to shake myself. There was nothing wrong with femininity or feminine magic. There certainly wasn't anything wrong with self-love. I swallowed.

"Thanks Mom," I said, and tried to mean it. "It's beautiful."

"Try it on!" she urged. "I got it from this great little shop on Etsy—Rhiannon got me into Etsy and now I can't stop buying things! There are so many possibilities."

"Yeah," I said.

I fiddled with the clasp, but it was easier not to argue.

I slipped it on and did up the clasp at the back of my neck. It hung just below my collarbone, over my sweater.

"It's beautiful," Grandma said. "Now if only we could get you in a nicer shirt…"

"I'm comfortable," I said tersely. "And it's Christmas." My clothes weren't really that bad—a baggy sweater with holes at the cuff and collar, and jeans. No one else was dressed much nicer, except they all wore soft shades of green and brown, and there was a staggering amount of floral applique.

"Do you want to look at it?" Mom asked.

"I'm okay," I said quickly. "I saw it in the box." I undid the clasp and put it away again. "Thank you," I repeated, because that was what I was supposed to say.

"I want to open another one!" Misty announced, saving me. I leaned over to the tree and passed her something quickly.

I ENDED UP on the couch next to Brian. He was a good-natured man who was as much of a nature-loving hippie as the rest of the family, and he seemed to have taken the "witch" thing in stride. I didn't know him well, but I liked him. He didn't feel the need to fill a space with chatter, but as long as I was next to him, I looked like I was socializing.

Grandma took the chair nearest me. Even seated, she gave off a vaguely critical aura.

"I heard you've been taking hormone supplements," she said.

"Oh, didn't you notice?" I asked dryly.

She gave me a sharp look.

I waved at my chin.

Brian made a quiet huffing noise.

"What are the side effects?" she asked.

"Besides all the hair, you mean?"

"I mean the risks. You know it's not healthy to put extra hormones in your body, especially ones that aren't supposed to be there."

"I'm supposed to have testosterone in my body," I said. "I feel better with it."

"You know what I mean," she said. She never raised her voice, but she had the imperious tone of a weary professor. "You have a perfectly good body, and you think you know better what you can put into it. There's just no evidence of what the long-term side effects are. I worry about you."

"My doctor has a pretty good idea what the risks are." She also knew what the risks of not getting treatment were, but I didn't like to bring up suicide statistics at family lunches. It didn't feel right, and it would quickly get me more patholo-gized than I already was. I wasn't going to bring up the risks of vaginal atrophy right now, either. I knew about it, I had talked to my doctor about it, and my grandmother didn't need to know. It would only prove her point.

"Doctors don't know everything," she said. "They're putting kids on hormones too, and that's not safe."

I couldn't stop the sigh that gusted out of me. "No one is putting kids on HRT. They're using puberty blockers, which are perfectly safe and have been used by cis kids for decades. Besides, I'm not a kid. I'm an adult who talked to my doctor, and we decided this was the best choice for me."

"You're so young," she said. "I wish you could have waited."

"Well, I couldn't." I glanced around the room looking for a distraction. Rhiannon and Misty had disappeared, and Hazel and Mom seemed deep in discussion about something. Brian was sitting up, awake, listening, but even when I met his gaze, he didn't say anything.

"You have a lot of life left, and you'll understand you're being hasty. It's not fair, the way young women today are being told they're really men just because they want to be independent. I was an independent woman when I was twenty, and no one tried to say I was too manly."

"That's great for you," I said. I felt too hot, the wool of my sweater scratching me past bearing. I had to get away, now, before I yelled, before I heard anything that would damage our relationship past fixing. "I'm not a woman. That's all it is. This isn't some political statement—" My voice climbed.

Mom and Hazel stilled their conversation, their eyes on me.

"I understand that you feel that way," Grandma said. "I want you to do what makes you happy."

"Great," I said. "So you understand why I did this, then."

"But you could have been happy as a woman. There's nothing wrong with being a woman."

There was no way to explain this to people who didn't want to understand. It was true that there was nothing wrong with being a woman. I wished I could have been happy that way. I had given up so much to come out, but talking about that nuance would only make them think they had won.

I stood up. "I'm going for a walk."

"You can't leave in the middle of a conversation," Grandma said sharply.

"The conversation is over," I said. "I don't have to justify my existence to you."

"Don't snap at me," she said. "I'm trying to understand."

"I have to go." I turned and stormed toward the door.

Mom stood too. "Hon—"

"Don't." This time I really did snap, and she snatched her hand back like I had screamed. No one else tried to stop me as I grabbed my coat and fled out the door and into the snow.

Chapter Eight

I WAS HALFWAY down Main Street before it occurred to me that
nothing would be open. In Portland, there was always something open within walking distance—an ampm or Jack In The
Box if nothing else. But it was 4 p.m. on Christmas, and that
meant the whole town was shuttered. The Jack In The Box
glowed faintly by the highway, but I was pretty sure it would be
closed, and even if it wasn't, sitting alone in there would make
me feel even worse than sitting with my family.

The light in The Three Pines was on.

I stood at the picture window and stared in, head spinning.
It felt like a hallucination that it could be open and welcoming
when I needed it most. It was the kind of thing that only happened in cheesy movies that lacked conflict.

The Christmas tree inside was lit, the electric fire flickered,
and the "Open" sign glowed a welcoming orange.

Bea came out of the back with a bucket, and I stepped into
the shop.

She looked up. "Will," she said dazedly.

"Hi," I said, and my voice came out croaky.

She thunked the bucket down and came around the counter.
"Are you okay? I wasn't expecting to see you today."

"Yeah, well—" I thought I would be able to hold it together,
but her concern made my throat swell with unshed tears. "I

needed a break from my family. What are you doing here? Did your boss really make you work today?"

"Not exactly," she said. "He told me he'd pay me if I wanted to open, but I wasn't obligated."

The subtext sat between us. Either she, too, was avoiding her family, or she was desperate enough for money that she was sacrificing Christmas dinner with kin. She wore a bright-red sweater with a pattern of reindeer and earrings shaped like tree ornaments. She was so pretty, so perfectly dressed, that she didn't feel real. She put on such a good show.

"I'm sorry," I said lamely.

"We did dinner last night," she said airily, tucking a strand of hair behind her ear. "This way, I get to see you."

"Can't imagine I'm better company than a day off."

"Don't sell yourself short. Do you want to talk about it?"

I shrugged. "Was your dad mad, last night?" I asked instead.

She shrugged back. "I mean, yes, but it's fine. He just needs something to complain about."

"It shouldn't be you."

"I'm used to it," she said. "And it was Christmas. He wasn't being irrational."

"Was dinner nice?"

"It's always good," she said. "My mom pulls all the stops out for Christmas." She hesitated, then said softly, "She's been so depressed lately that she's barely been cooking, so it was nice to see her motivated."

"That's good," I said. It felt inadequate. I hadn't realized, and I didn't know how to provide comfort now. "I'm glad you got the night off to spend with her, then."

Bea nodded, then cleared her throat and took a step back.

"Do you want something to drink?"

"I suppose I should order something."

"Geoff would never know," she said. "We all drink so much espresso while we're working."

"I'm not going to come in, cry all over you, and not even support the establishment in which I do my crying."

"You haven't actually cried," she said. "You've barely even complained."

I didn't cry much anymore. Testosterone hadn't turned me angrier or hornier, but it had dried up my tears. I didn't even want to complain. It was the same bullshit as always. It was the same stuff I always faced when I went home. But I wanted Bea to know and understand me.

"Seeing you makes me feel better," I said. "I don't want to waste time with you talking about my family when we could be talking about anything else."

She nodded. "Well, I'm here for you. Go sit down; I'll make us some hot chocolate."

I did as she told me. The armchairs by the fire were toasty warm, and a half-finished puzzle was left on the table between them. I picked up a few pieces but made little progress before I abandoned them to watch Bea work. Christmas music played on the shop stereo, but it was soft and choral, easily ignorable. She moved around behind the counter efficiently, mixing our drinks and cleaning the counters and tidying up. She looked at home, competent and graceful. I settled into the chair as warmth spread through my stomach. I wanted to touch her, to get up and take the dish towel out of her hand and distract her entirely. I had tonight with her, and that would be all I could ask, but that at least could be good. Fun.

We deserved fun.

I pressed my palms together and waited.

She flicked off half the overhead lights, then crossed to the window, closed the blinds, and locked the door.

"You don't have to close for me," I said. "I'm not going to have an embarrassing meltdown."

"No one has come in in three hours," she said. "And you're right, I have better ways to spend my Christmas than working. Do you have any of that brandy left?"

I checked the inside pocket of my jacket, and the flask was still there. I handed it to her, and she added generous portions to both of the mugs, then handed me one. She took a seat in the other armchair and tucked her feet up under her.

"Well, merry Christmas," she said.

"Merry Christmas," I agreed with less bitterness than I expected. This felt like the ideal Christmas, I realized. Sitting in a quiet coffee shop with Bea when no one wanted anything from either of us. She was who I wanted; she made my days feel special.

"You sure you don't want to talk about it?"

What could I say? That Aunt Hazel's acceptance scared me as much as everyone else's concern? That I was half considering throwing my life away for Bea? That my family still thought I was a woman, and thought the things I did to my body were shameful and sickening?

I took a drink of hot chocolate. It was mostly alcohol. "It's just well-intended transphobia," I said. "They don't mean anything by it."

"Shouldn't they learn how not to be transphobic?"

"I guess," I said.

"I wish it was easier for you."

"Me too," I said. "I wish things were easier for both of us."

"I'm here with you now," she answered.

I nodded. Then, I put my drink down on the step by the fire. "I want to kiss you," I said. "I've been thinking about it all day."

"Here I was worried that I came on too strong last night."

"No," I said hastily. "No, I'm…I'm the one trying not to scare you off. I… You make me want to…" I swallowed.

"…bend me over the desk and have your way with me?"

I laughed. "You make me want to say poetic things about romance, and cook you dinner, and make you smile, and yes, bend you over my imaginary desk and touch every inch of you."

She took several deep breaths, and her chest heaved. I couldn't help the way my gaze dropped to the swell of her breasts, just hinted at through her sweater.

"If we start now, I think we can get through that whole list tonight," she said, and then she peeled her sweater off. Under it, she wore only a pale-green camisole, one cup of her bra peeking out. I took a deep breath of my own, and it didn't make me any less dizzy. She climbed into my armchair, mostly in my lap, and I put one hand on her waist and the other behind her head to draw her face down to mine.

The kiss was as head spinning as the last one, but less desperate, more sure. She slid her nails through the stubble on my chin and moaned in a way that went right to my dick. I shifted, spread my legs slightly, and drew my tongue along her lower lip. She tasted like brandy and chocolate, and I was more drunk from one kiss than I would have been even if I'd downed the whole flask. She melted into me, soft and warm, and my skin burned everywhere we touched.

Her hand against my cheek, my pinky finger against the sliver of exposed skin on her hip, our lips, our tongues.

I needed more.

I slid my hand under the hem of her camisole and pressed my palm to the small of her back, and she made a pleased gasp. Encouraged, I took her breast in hand and squeezed. Even through the padding of her bra, I could feel her nipple hardening, and when I swiped a thumb over the bud, she squirmed. I moved to pull her shirt off and stopped myself. I pulled back from the kiss too, but took a minute to stop fully, still pressing my lips to her half-closed mouth.

"We, um…we should stop now if we're going to stop."

"I don't want to," she said.

"Me neither, but we're in public."

"I locked the door, and it's dumping snow out there. No one's going to come in."

"Security cameras?" I asked.

Her laughter vibrated across my lips. "Those cost money."

"Okay," I said. I glanced over her shoulder to check the curtains, but they were firmly shut, and the lights were dim enough that anyone walking by would assume the shop was closed.

"I left my cock at home," I warned. "I hope that's okay."

She hummed. "You know what they say—'country girls make do.'"

I laughed and tugged her so she straddled my lap. Then I slid her camisole and bra straps off in one movement and shoved them down to her waist. Her pale breasts glowed in the light from the fire, her nipples pebbled to hardness. I took one in my mouth and the other in my hand, and she groaned in response and grabbed the back of my head, pressing my face closer to her. I obeyed her cues, rolling her nipple between my lips and pulling back to slide my soft tongue across it. She writhed, and

I pressed one hand to her back so when she bucked her hips, she would have more friction.

"Will," she groaned. "*Will.*"

I only moved my mouth to her other nipple. Her hand clenched, tugging at my hair. I pressed my hand to the button on her jeans, then hesitated.

"Can I?"

"God, yes," she gasped. Then, "No, not yet."

I pulled my hand back.

"You're fully dressed," she said. "And I'm—" She bucked her hips again.

I could get off without taking a single article of clothing off, and sometimes I preferred it that way. I wouldn't need to expose my body to her, could let her keep living the fantasy of what she thought I looked like under the armor of sweater and binder and stubble.

"I'm in no hurry," I lied.

"I am," she said, and tugged at my sweater.

I took a deep breath. "I'll undress myself," I said. "Give me a little space."

She bit her lip, and I thought about running. I reminded myself that any awkwardness would be worth it if I got to keep kissing her.

She slid off my lap. "Hold on a second," she said. She pulled off her top and then hurried into the back room. I took the moment to collect myself; she returned with a few towels that she laid down on the rug.

Her tits bounced as she shimmied out of her jeans, her nipples still flushed from my touches, and I forgot I was supposed to be undressing myself as I got caught up in watching her.

My dick was so hard it ached, and when I moved to stand it dragged against the seam of my jeans. I clenched my jaw.

She took a half step toward me, then twisted her hands together. I sighed and stripped my sweater off.

"You don't have to," she said, "if you're more comfortable staying dressed. But I want you—as much of you as you're willing to give me."

I didn't hate my body, was the thing. I loved my body, loved every change that affirmed who I was. Every shot I put into my ass made the person I saw in the mirror feel more like me. But I was always intensely aware that I was being watched, that the changes were being cataloged by those around me, and that I would never be man enough for some people.

I could keep my clothes on and delay the reckoning, but I only had another day with Bea, and I had to know now. I couldn't spend the next months wondering how things might have gone.

There was no graceful way to take off a binder, so I peeled it over my head with as much dignity as I could manage, aware of Bea's gaze burning through me. I didn't want to think about her potential judgment, so I bought myself a few more seconds by stripping down entirely before I looked back at her. My breasts had grown soft from years of T and binding, and hair now grew down my sternum and across my belly, but there was no hiding what my first puberty had done to me. Bea's gaze flicked across me and away.

"You can look," I said.

I wanted her to see me.

I wanted her to love my body for what it was.

"I don't want you to feel like I'm staring," she said. "I expect people do a lot of that around you."

I cleared my throat and tried to find an answer. Yes, and no. I wasn't hot enough to be noticed by people attracted to men, was finally masculine enough to go unnoticed by people attracted to women, and so I was invisible. Until, of course, I came out, and the questions about surgeries started.

Somehow, Bea hadn't asked a single question all week. I was relieved, but I also wanted to share myself with her. She was the one person I wouldn't mind asking questions, and it was because she didn't ask them. It was a contradiction I wasn't sure I would ever be able to reconcile.

"It's different when it's you," I said. "It's different when I'm being seen as me, not as some freak of medicine."

"Being trans isn't—"

"I know," I said quickly. "But I see the way people look at me."

She nodded and sat down, then beckoned me forward with her hands. "I want to touch you," she said.

I wanted to be touched. I knelt to kiss her, and she pulled me down until we lay side by side, still slowly exploring. Her hand slid up my side and stopped on my rib cage.

"I've never been with a trans guy," she said. "So you'll have to tell me what you like."

"Same stuff most guys like," I said. "The equipment's all the same, it just isn't standard-issue sizing."

"You have a bespoke body," she said, and then kissed me. I resisted the urge to roll her onto her back and pick up where I had left off. I wanted to be touching her, and I wanted to be in control, but I had to let her be an equal participant.

She seemed determined to explore every inch of me; between kisses, she ran her hands over my jawline, my collarbone, down my sternum. Slowly, gently, her nails tickled through the faint dusting of hair on my chest and then through the thicker hair on my belly. I kept answering her kisses, kept my hand against her hip, tried to keep myself still for her.

Hesitantly, she ran her palm down the outside of my hip and then the inside of my thigh.

"You're so hairy," she said, softly enough that I couldn't judge her tone.

"Sorry," I said, to be safe.

"I like it," she said. "You're…" She trailed off.

"What?"

"I love your body. Is that cheesy to say? It feels right to me."

My body wasn't for anyone but me, except that in this moment, I got to share it, and that felt magical. I shifted so I was propped on one hip and kissed her, then trailed my fingers along her ribcage so she shivered. "Yours is pretty spectacular too," I answered.

She grabbed a fistful of my hair and held me to her, and I decided the gentle exploration was over. I rolled her to her back and kissed her neck, then slid my fingers through her slick folds. She let out a high, breathy gasp as I brushed against her clit.

"Do you want me inside?" I asked.

"Yes," she groaned.

I rubbed her clit slowly, feeling her flush and thicken under my thumb, and then pressed a finger inside her. Her hand tightened in my hair.

I'd never been good at talking during sex, but her small "Please" told me a lot without her needing to ask. As I pumped my finger into her, she pressed up, drawing me deeper.

"More, Will," she begged, and I obliged, pressing a second

finger in, quickening my pace, still rubbing at her clit with my thumb. I could tell she was close when her breathing began to stutter, and I kissed her so that when she came around me; her groan echoed through my mouth. She clenched down several times before I pulled out and drew back.

She blinked slowly at the ceiling, a look of grave consideration on her face. I snuggled up against her, the whole of my chest flush with her side, and asked, "You okay?"

"Yeah," she said. "I'm good. Just let me..." She sighed and tilted her head so our cheeks pressed together too. "I feel so good," she said in my ear. "Like nothing could ever hurt me again."

It should have been too much, too romantic, too intense.

"I got you," I said instead. "I'll protect you."

She rolled against me and slid a hand between my legs. Her fingers circled the tip of my dick. I groaned and buried my face in her shoulder.

She made a noise that sounded like surprise and kept rubbing, more insistently. I hitched a knee up over her thigh, giving her more access. When her fingers moved to tease at my slit, I shook my head against her shoulder.

"Not there," I said. I didn't like being penetrated.

"Okay," she answered, and moved her touch back to my dick. It felt so different to let someone else touch me, vulnerable and heightened. I couldn't be quite sure what she would do next, though just her gentle rubbing was enough to tighten coils of pleasure through my entire core. I slipped a hand between us and pressed her closer, so she moved more insistently.

"God," I mumbled.

She hesitated.

"Don't stop," I said quickly. "You feel so good, and I'm so

close—"

She stroked me faster, and I thrust into her hand until all the tension inside me evaporated and waves of pleasure washed through me. I gasped for breath, the sound muffled by her skin, and kept my hand against hers until I came down.

"Was that okay?" she asked, her voice very soft.

I laughed into her shoulder. "Okay? Jesus. Yes."

I rolled away and ran my fingers through my hair. A wave of exhaustion flowed through me. I could have happily fallen asleep right there on the rug.

"God damn," I said, and laughed weakly. "Did we really just do that?"

"I thought you wanted to."

"I meant, did we really just do that on the floor of a coffee shop?"

"Where else would we have done it? You have eight hundred people in your house, and I couldn't bring you home."

I didn't miss the slight hesitation in her voice when she said that. "Would your parents mind about me?"

It wasn't the right thing to ask in the moment when we were both still warm and sated from the afterglow and the firelight, giddy with each other. I shouldn't have asked. I was leaving town tomorrow, and that would be the end of it.

I shouldn't have had sex with her at all, because now I knew enough to miss her with specificity.

"Not really," she said. "They're well-meaning but ignorant, so they'll probably say something painful and stupid, but they won't be…you know. But I told them I was working until five, and their feelings would be hurt if they thought I was lying to them."

I hummed in acknowledgment. She laid her head on my shoulder and trailed her fingers up and down my side. My eyes blinked shut, and the only sounds in the room were her breathing and the crackles of the electric fireplace.

"Okay," she said abruptly, and my eyes snapped open. "We can't fall asleep here, and I need to clean up before we leave."

I sat up and reached for my clothes. She was right, and I wished she wasn't. I wished she was in my bed. I wished I could do this with her tomorrow, in privacy and peace. I watched her pull her clothes on and wished I didn't feel like I was counting down seconds.

Chapter Nine

EVERYONE WAS STILL awake when I let myself into the house. I had been hoping to wait until past bedtime, but Bea had a schedule to keep, and I couldn't wander around in the dark and snowy town for hours without risking exhaustion and hyperthermia.

Mom looked up when I came in. Her eyes slid over me, and she returned to the sink of dirty dishes. So it was going to be like that. My mouth formed the apologies that were as natural to me as hunger and sleep, the familiar necessities of life.

I'm sorry for yelling. I'm sorry for ruining Christmas. I'm sorry for running away and not being who you want.

We would stay in combat until one of us apologized, and the chances were good that it would be me.

"Your grandmother has gone home," she said coldly.

"Okay," I answered flatly.

"You hurt her feelings."

"Well, she hurt mine."

"You have to be patient with her. She wants what's best for you. We all do."

"I believe you," I said. It was the only concession I could make. Guilt welled up in me. I had a family who loved me, who tried to support me. They failed, but they meant well.

Could I live with that? Giving up on the euphoria of community to go back to a life with people who only tolerated me? I should have been able to. I should have more grace in my heart.

"You should visit her and apologize on your way out of town tomorrow," she said.

I thought about it. It didn't need to mean anything—it was just words, to keep the family peace. To keep things quiet.

"Will she apologize to me?" I asked instead, and even I was shocked by how bitter my voice was. Despite the guilt, despite wishing I could be a kind, forgiving saint—someone who could let the ignorance roll off my back—apparently I was fresh out of grace.

"She was just asking questions."

"For fuck's sake, Mom," I breathed out.

"Don't take that tone with me," she snapped.

"Not interrogating people about their medical history is a pretty basic rule of common decency. All the information about transitioning is out there if you were willing to google it. But none of you have put in the slightest fucking effort to learn who I am."

"Because you didn't talk to me! You just dumped all of this on me and ran away to another state, like you always—"

"Didn't it occur to you—?" My voice cracked, but the tears didn't come. "I was trying to figure out who I was, too, and I needed some space. You just expect me to know everything, and forgive you for every misstep, and be the bigger person?"

"You didn't give me the chance!"

"I was seventeen," I said. "I couldn't—I had to learn all of this on my own. And you just sit up here with your 'good vibes' bullshit and expect education to drop into your lap. I was scared, and I wanted my mom, and you made this about you and what you had lost!"

"Hon—" For a second, concern flickered across her face, as if something I'd said had gotten through.

I was too angry to let it affect me. "My name is Will," I snarled. "But you can't even manage that."

"Don't—"

"I'm sleeping at Hazel's," I said, and stormed out of the room.

HAZEL'S WAS A mile away, and it took me half an hour to get there through the thick slush piled by the highway. I arrived at her house soggy, exhausted, and embarrassed.

Hazel took one look at me and pulled me into a tight hug. "I'm sorry," she said. "Have you been walking around in the snow this whole time?"

"No," I said quickly. "Went to the coffee shop, then back to Mom's, then…couldn't stay."

She rubbed my back, then said, "Let me make you a cup of tea."

I followed her into the kitchen, shoulders hunched around my ears like some sort of pathetic stray cat. Her three dogs pressed around me, sniffing me with suspicion.

"I'm sorry I didn't intervene," she said. "I didn't realize…"

"It's fine," I said numbly. "You're not obliged to police your mother's language."

"It's not fair that the burden of education falls on you," she said. "We could all do better."

It was so close to what I had said to Mom that I couldn't argue, so I stayed quiet. Hazel made us both mugs of chamomile tea and sat down at the table.

"I know you know that your grandmother loves you," she said.

"Yeah," I said, and my heart sank. I didn't know why I thought this would be any different. Hazel might have lived in Seattle for a decade, but she still came back here. She still decided that her family and the magic of the woods mattered more than the freedom of a queer community. She'd asked me to move back for a reason, and she clearly thought it was the best path for me. I braced for an argument.

"Sometimes, people can't love us the way we deserve."

I flinched and spilled hot water down my hand. "What do you mean?"

"I mean that you can take your grandmother's love, and be grateful that you have it, and know it hurts more than it heals."

That was it exactly. I knew my family loved me. I knew my mom loved me. But every way they chose to express it hurt me, asked me to be someone I wasn't.

"Yeah," I said. "It's one thing when they call on birthdays, but every day like this…"

I could tell other people that they never had to come out to their parents or that they could live without their parents' love. But thinking about losing my family's love still hurt.

"Mom won't use my name," I said. It felt like betraying her to even say it out loud, to admit her faults. She had tried so hard, she loved me so much, and she couldn't even do that.

"I know," Hazel said. "I want to say she'll learn better, but I think all I can say is that she loves you. I know how much. But you can decide that isn't enough for you."

"Doesn't that make me ungrateful?" I said. "There are so many people who get disowned by their families, who get kicked out of their homes—"

"There's more to life than black-and-white morality," Hazel said. "Even a coven like ours, that claims to only practice white magic, can be petty and vindictive to those outside our circle."

I smiled weakly. There were a lot of stories of hexes on ex-boyfriends, the kinds of small magic that meant they would never have matching socks or parking spots.

"I want..." I wanted so much. I wanted to come home and feel safe. I wanted to wake up every morning and see mountains.

I wanted Bea.

I couldn't have any of it. I didn't understand how people could love me so much and hurt me so badly.

"Why did you ask me to come live with you?" I asked. My voice came out small and scared.

"Because I love you," she said. "And you're quiet, and responsible, and I trust you. And when you call me, you don't sound happy. If you want to come home, you'll have a place with me, and I'll take care of you. It seems like you're always working, and you don't need to be. You have family. But Will, I don't expect you to. I understand if you decide it's not what will make you happy."

I wish I knew what would make me happy.

I took a drink of tea and tried to think. I wanted to come home, but the home I wanted to return to didn't and had never existed. "You know I can't," I said.

She nodded. "It was nice to hope. But I didn't want to live here when I was in my twenties either."

"You didn't?"

She looked startled. "Goddess, no. Why do you think I have a PhD?"

"I thought you liked being in school."

"I did. And I liked going on dates, and getting Vietnamese food at midnight, and walking to the grocery store."

"So why did you come back?"

"I missed my coven, and my sisters. They were having children who I wanted to help raise. Eventually, those things mattered more. Also, rent in Seattle was fucking expensive even in the '80s."

I laughed. That was true. But it didn't matter how cheap rent was in Serendipity if there were no jobs.

"You can come back later, if you decide to," Hazel said, "or if there's someone worth coming back for." I narrowed my eyes at her, and she shrugged. "Hypothetically."

"Hypothetically," I agreed, but I could no longer imagine it. I would lose too much.

I WOKE UP to a text.

Betty Draper
Good morning sunshine 😊 Pancakes or waffles?

I stared at it for a long time, and my chest hurt. I shouldn't reply, but I could break up with someone without being a dick about it.

Me
A real man eats only protein for breakfast.

Betty Draper
RIP to men's arteries. I prefer to rot my teeth with sugar.

I had to walk back to Mom's and apologize and pack my things before I could see Bea. None of that would be fun, but it would put off the goodbyes for an hour or two. A miserable hour without coffee, but it was worth something.

I dislodged myself from the nest of blankets in front of the heater, displacing the dog who had chosen to spend the night with me, and gathered my clothes to my chest. No one was up yet, which meant no one had to see me out of my binder and be reminded of how my body was shaped. I locked myself in the bathroom and showered, which woke me up a little bit. Twelve more hours and I would be back in my studio apartment with my espresso machine and stacks of books and freedom to walk around shirtless.

The sun was just barely up, blindingly bright on the fresh snow. I watched a deer pick its way across the front garden with a pang. It was beautiful, with an enormous rack of antlers. It turned, and met my eyes, and blinked slowly. I stayed perfectly still, hoping that I wouldn't spook it.

Then, he shook his head and bounded back into the woods.

I let out the breath I had been holding. I was past ascribing meanings to nature when my mind was made up, but it was still a wonderful sight.

Hazel tromped across the yard in a winter coat and knee-high boots along an already-cleared path. She carried an armload of chopped wood. I hurried to the front door and let her in.

She nodded her thanks and pulled her scarf down from over her mouth.

"You really shouldn't be hauling wood with your bad knee," I admonished.

"You let me worry about that," she said. "How did you sleep?"

"Your floors are very hard," I said. "That's what I get for throwing a tantrum late at night. Why don't you have wood stacked on your porch?"

"I ran out," she said. "I'll make someone haul more for me once they're awake."

Guilt filled my throat. I should have stayed. Bea would have stayed, because Bea was a better person than I was.

"I'll do it," I said.

"Nonsense. Someone else will wake up soon, and you need to drive home today."

"It won't take me long," I said. "And it will let me put off talking to Mom."

Hazel raised an eyebrow, but she didn't argue.

I pulled on my Doc Martens, which were freezing cold and still damp from my trek the night before. My gloves at least were proper cold-weather gear, and I owned a decent raincoat.

I was sweaty and exhausted by the time I finished hauling a day's worth of wood, and my hair was frozen. I leaned against the closed door and shed my layers, trying to cool down. My ribs strained against my binder, and it took a minute to get my breath back.

"Well, I'm awake now," I said, though I kind of wanted to go back to bed.

"Thank you, sweetheart," Hazel said. "Do you want eggs?"

I nodded. "Does the plow come up this far?"

"What do you think?" she asked, and I groaned. I would need to walk back to Mom's.

I LET MYSELF into Mom's house without knocking. I was hoping I could sneak past her, but she was sitting at the kitchen table. We stared at each other for a minute. I wasn't expecting an apology, but I didn't want to apologize either.

Boundaries. Personal responsibility. Being the bigger person.

I was tired of being the bigger person.

"I'm not going to apologize to Grandma," I announced. "I made my boundaries clear, and she didn't listen to them."

"She's old—"

"I've heard all the excuses. I've made them all for her myself. You don't have to guilt-trip me, I'm more than capable of doing it to myself. But I'm tired of it. I love you, and I love her, but I'm not going to be near people who don't see me for who I am anymore."

"I don't guilt-trip."

I bit back a petulant response. "I'm happy with my life," I lied. "I like who I am. I know who I am. If I'm going to keep seeing you, I need you to trust that I'm making the right decisions for myself."

"Hon, you know it's just because we worry."

"Don't make excuses." My voice cracked. "Don't act like— like I'm making a mistake." I thought I had this all figured out. I'd had the whole walk back from Aunt Hazel's to think about what I would say.

I was so scared to ask for what I needed because not getting it would be like getting rejected all over again. I just wanted them to trust me. I wrapped my arms around myself, and my nails bit into the skin of my arms.

"I know you're smart," she said, "but I can't help it. I'm your mother, and I was never prepared to worry about a—son."

I didn't miss the hitch in her voice.

"It's not an insult to say I'm trans," I said. "It's the truth."

"Honey, you know I love and accept you no matter what. I've always loved gay people—my sister is a lesbian! You act like I'm some bigot, but you know I'm not."

"If you're so open minded, say my name."

"I don't understand."

"You haven't said my name all week," I said. "You go out of your way to avoid it."

Her hands fluttered over the table nervously. "I must have said it."

"I would have noticed."

"I'm not trying to be hurtful. It's just hard for me. I picked out your name for you, and you threw it away."

"Okay," I said, and turned to go upstairs.

"Will," she said, and I froze. I wanted it to feel like acceptance, or at least like relief. I wanted it to be enough.

I didn't feel any better.

I didn't feel much of anything.

"Don't walk away," she begged. "I want to understand."

"Not enough," I said, and I went upstairs.

Chapter Ten

By the time I had escaped into my car, the snowplow had come through and the roads were clear. I could have made it back to the highway in five minutes and been on my way home. I was all used up, and the thought of another confrontation terrified me. I'd ghosted more than my fair share of dates in the past, but Bea deserved more.

I still sat in front of the only diner in town for fifteen minutes, fighting down tears. Stupid, I thought. Stupid and worthless, couldn't even talk to a pretty girl the way she deserved. Wasn't brave enough.

I slammed the door behind me and saw her rusted blue truck on the other side of the street. It filled me with dread.

Bea already had two cups of coffee in front of her when I came in. The Moonlight Diner was weirdly empty for the Sunday after Christmas, but apparently Serendipity valued family togetherness more than brunch. When I slid into the small booth across from Bea, she reached out and squeezed my hand. Her eyes were shining.

She didn't ask about my family, for which I was grateful. "Look at this!" she squealed and slid her phone to me with the notification screen up. I scrolled through a dozen notifications from "Sell on Etsy."

Amy bought something from your shop.
Rose bought something from your shop.

A guest bought something from your shop.

"This is great," I said. "Is it a lot?"

"They started coming in about 5 a.m.," she said. "East Coast morning. I must have been featured on a blog or Pinterest or something, because I've never sold so much in one day."

"That's amazing!" I replied. I was thrilled for her and thrilled for a distraction. "Congratulations! So you're buying breakfast?"

"Nice try, hotshot," she laughed. "I still don't wear a tie to work. But this is really nice. If it keeps up for a couple days, I might be able to fix the heater in the truck. Or I could buy something that gets better gas mileage. Either way, I need to go home after this and make another batch just in case I stay popular through the spring."

The waitress came to take our orders. I picked quickly, thinking more about Bea's store. I didn't know what the profit margins on soap were, but my head was already turning ideas over. "Are blogs and Pinterest the main way Etsy stores get publicity?" I asked when we were alone again. "There must be more traditional forms of advertising available to you."

"Are you going to design a commercial for me?"

"I don't do commercials," I said. "I do fancy tweets for cheap toys. But it must be the same principle."

"You've already done enough for me," she said. "You're the reason any of this is happening."

"I am?"

"Your prosperity jar. I took it out last night and burned the candle before bed, and I woke up to this."

She'd succeeded because she had built a shop and put in the hard work and hoped and advertised and made good product. That was more reliable than any spell. Magic never claimed to be a substitute for any of those things, only a boost.

"That's all on you," I said. "You're the one who built a shop worth promoting."

"And you promoted it," she said, smiling in the way that made my heart jump to my throat. I wanted to lean across the table and kiss her. I swallowed and put my hands on my lap.

"I'm so happy for you," I said. "I hope you sell every bar in your inventory."

"Me too," she said. "I feel like I need to design more scents, and a spring line, and maybe new packaging, before I send out so many, but I don't want to get ahead of myself. It all takes money, and I don't know if this is a fluke or not."

"How do you decide what kind of soap to make?" I asked.

I let her talk for a while about different chemical compositions and the best molds and dyes and expanding to lotions and body butters. I probably had a stupid smile on my face, but she was so earnest that it was hard to control myself. Talking about her shop lit her up, and I wanted to do whatever it took to keep her excited about it.

Our pancakes came, and when the waitress left, Bea ducked her head. "Sorry," she said. "This is probably boring, huh?"

"Not at all," I assured her. "First of all, I get paid to describe plastic dinosaurs, so if we're competing for boring jobs, I win. Second of all, I think it's great that you know all of this, and I'm enjoying learning about it. Third, I love to hear how experts describe things because it's always more interesting than an outsider's opinion."

She blushed and stared at her coffee. "We really don't have to talk about me. How's your mom?"

"I *want* to talk about you," I said, and then regretted it. It was the truth. I wanted to talk to her about anything and everything forever. But it felt a bit like leading her on, even though friends talked about their jobs all the time.

She pressed her knee against mine under the table, and heat rushed up the inside of my thigh.

"It seems early to plan for spring soaps," I said, trying to drag my mind back to her shop and away from her touch. "Surely you have a little time."

"It takes six weeks to cure the soap," she said, "and I have to order supplies and wait for them to ship…" She was off again. I reached out and took her hand and kept listening.

Eventually, she slowed down and looked down at our joined hands. "I'm sorry," she said again. "I'm just talking about myself."

"Bea," I said seriously. "You deserve to talk about yourself. You have interesting things to say, and there are people who want to listen."

She shrugged.

"I—" Oh Goddess, this was going to be terrible. I was going to be an asshole. I was going to look like a liar by the end of this. "Your soap is valuable because you care about it, but it's also something that people in cities would lose their minds over. Everyone there wants handmade, hand crafted, organic, all that sort of stuff. They aren't stuck shopping at Fred Meyer for everything, and they want to think they're better than their friends because they're supporting local artisans. There's a way to take your soap's value and sell it to people."

"I have to get it to the cities though."

"I know," I said. "But that's— I'm not— It's not about the soap for me. It's about you, and learning what you're excited about, and what you like and why. It makes me excited. You light up when you smile."

"Just wait," she said. "My parents are so sick of me talking about scent blends and packaging, they just leave the room when I start."

It was clearly meant to be a funny story, and it really wasn't. I floundered for something to say in response that wasn't "Fuck your parents."

"Well," I said slowly, "Maybe you need better parents."

She smiled ruefully. "I don't have anywhere to exchange them, and I usually like them."

I was, maybe, a bit defensive. I also hadn't seen anything that endeared her parents to me in the last week. I sighed and sat back in my booth. "Clearly some people care," I said, and gestured at her phone. "It isn't the same thing, but it's something."

I wanted to tell her to leave her family behind, cut ties, reinvent herself. Not everyone was ready for the drastic action that I was, and I hadn't been ready for it a week ago. I still didn't want to go scorched earth on my family, or issue ultimatums, or cut them off. I just needed space.

"It's something," she agreed, but she looked sad.

I took a too-large bite of waffle to buy myself time and stop myself from pushing. Denial was a powerful drug, and she was still stuck in it. Life was easier when you told yourself that everyone was doing their best, that disinterest was the best you deserved. When all you were used to was empty rituals, you didn't know how much magic you were missing in your life. I couldn't make Bea wake up and notice it without being pushy. She had to come to that conclusion on her own.

The conversation moved on to gentler topics while we ate our way through a mountain of breakfast food and my chest grew tighter and tighter. When I had put my credit card on the table to pay, I said, "I don't think we should try to make long distance work."

She dropped her fork. "Excuse me?"

"I can't get out of Portland very often," I said. "I work all the time, and it's a long drive, and you work weekends…"

"Are you breaking up with me?" she asked. "I didn't even realize we were dating."

"I mean, we sure acted like it this week, and this—" I gestured between us.

"This didn't have to feel like a date," she said. "You're the reason it does."

"You acted like it was a date too!"

"Yes, because I thought it was the start of something." Her nostrils flared. "If I had known you were planning to cut it off when your Hallmark holiday was over, I wouldn't have bothered."

I hadn't expected anger from her. She didn't seem like an angry person even when she talked about her parents, but now her jaw was set as she glared at me. Maybe she didn't have a lifetime of swallowing anger and knowing she would be punished for it. Good.

"I like spending time with you," I said. "I'm your friend."

"I don't see how we can be friends when we both know that's not what we want."

"I don't want you expecting something from me that I can't give."

She sat back and crossed her arms. "So you're not even going to try."

"I live six hours away," I said firmly. "I can't come visit, and I can't ask you to come to me."

"You already did."

"Once. Once isn't enough to make a relationship work."

"Well, since you're the expert, I guess we should let you make all the decisions."

"That's not fair—"

"No, don't. If you're not willing to put the work in, then we *should* call it quits now. I don't want to be the only one putting in the emotional labor."

"That's not fair either."

"Neither is dumping me the morning after we had sex," she hissed, just as the waitress returned with my card. I signed the receipt, face hot.

"I'm sorry," I said, keeping my voice as low as possible. "I wanted to—but I was lying to myself. You deserve better than this. Don't—"

"I guess I do," she said, and stood.

"Bea—"

"Don't," she said, and her voice cracked. "I don't want to argue with you. If you're just going to run away, I'm not going to chase you." She scrambled for her coat and purse, then stormed outside half dressed.

I sat in the booth for what felt like a long time, gathering the energy to step outside too. I caught the waitress eying me surreptitiously and reached for my coat. I could have a breakdown in the privacy of my car instead of for the entertainment of the town.

Chapter Eleven

No one worked much the week between Christmas and New Year's. That should have been a nice break, but all it did was give me time to stew. I wanted to text Bea, to apologize, to see how she was doing. But I had done the dumping, and I knew I wasn't allowed. She got to decide if we stayed friends, and I had to respect that. All I could do was scroll through her Instagram (mostly inactive) and her Etsy page (every time I checked, another scent of soap had sold out).

So I moped through work, drove home in a haze, ate takeout, and went to bed without ever seeing daylight. I knew it wasn't helping my mental state, but it was satisfying to wallow.

Everyone I knew was busy, either with family or with working overtime to avoid family, and I didn't want to see them anyway. I didn't want to explain, or justify, or even share what I had dealt with. I knew Juniper would understand what had happened with my mom, but the thought of trying to talk about that made me want to go back to bed.

Unfortunately, I couldn't skip our New Year's Eve party without broadcasting to everyone that I was teetering close to a depressive pit that threatened to suck me under.

Juniper's household was throwing the party this year because the six people sharing their house had free reign of it. I arrived to a storm of glitter and streamers, and then Jay blew a noise-maker in my face and pressed a drink into my hand. I forced a smile on my face.

"This seems even more festive than usual," I said.

"Fuck 2021," Jay said cheerfully. "I'm going to make '22 my bitch."

I laughed. "Hell yeah," I said, though I didn't feel it at all.

Jay didn't seem to notice, and then the doorbell rang again, and he turned to open the door.

I found Juniper in the kitchen, swearing at the oven.

"Can I help?"

"Can you make this piece of shit bake at a consistent temperature?" They pushed their tangle of curls out of their face impatiently.

"I'm sure it will taste great," I said. "What are you making?"

"It will not," they seethed. "A chocolate soufflé needs to bake just right or it won't be fluffy enough." They pushed the rack back in the oven and turned. "Oh, good, you already got a drink. What did you bring to eat?"

I put my tray of deviled eggs on the counter and took the lid off. In the living room, someone put on music. I stayed in the kitchen while Juniper fought the oven; when they won, they worried over their extensive appetizer spread, then mixed another bowl of punch that looked to be more booze than juice.

"How was Christmas?" they asked. "I didn't hear from you all weekend."

I shrugged. "I think I'm done visiting my mom for a while."

They grimaced, but they didn't say "I told you so." Instead they said, "I'm sure by next year you'll have the fortitude to grin and bear it for six more days."

"Maybe," I said, dragging my fingers through the condensation on the outside of my punch glass. Juniper dumped a bag of powdered sugar into the electric mixer and turned it on. I waited for them to be done mixing to say, "I met someone."

They slammed their hands on the counter. "And you didn't tell me?"

"It didn't last."

"And?"

I sighed, "And I didn't want to talk about it." I still didn't, but I needed to. I wished I could keep it bottled up inside and wait for the pain to pass, but I knew from long experience that all that did was let me ruminate on the same anger until the wound turned septic.

I spilled out a summary of my week, skipping over the Solstice ritual and the details of our hookup, while Juniper interjected with the occasional curse and fussed over their leaning soufflé.

"So, I told her I didn't want to do long distance," I said, "and I came back."

"But you miss her."

"Yes."

"Even though you only went on one date and barely know her."

"Well...yes."

They sighed and rolled their eyes. "You met someone who makes you absolutely twitterpated, and then you decided the occasional drive is too much of an obstacle?"

When they put it like that, it sounded stupid. "It's not just the drive," I said. "It's that I can't go back to the town where my mom lives and avoid her, and I can't see her right now."

"Bullshit," they said. "You drive one of the most generic cars in the Pacific Northwest. Just don't park it anywhere obvious and you'll be fine."

"I don't think you realize how small Serendipity is," I said, "or how rural. My Prius sticks out, and if a single person saw me, they would mention it to Mom. I'm already the town freak."

"So fuck it," they said as they finally took the soufflé out of the oven. "If your Mom finds out, she'll figure out pretty quick why you aren't telling her you're there. You already told her where to shove it."

"It would hurt her feelings," I said lamely.

They didn't even justify that with a response.

I sucked down more extremely strong punch and worked through the fear churning in my gut. I couldn't set boundaries. I could whine and pout and occasionally get mad enough to yell, but I had never actually said "no" to my mom before. I had run away. I had ducked my head.

I had already told her what I needed, I realized. I had told her how to love me. It just didn't feel like it because I didn't trust her to listen.

"I ran away again," I said.

"You ran away again," Juniper agreed. "I can't act all high-and-mighty because I've ghosted about a hundred first dates, but if you like this girl so much, you're going to have to stand your ground."

"It doesn't matter," I said glumly. "She doesn't want to leave, and I don't want to go back. I want a relationship that feels like it's going somewhere."

"So go," they said. "Jesus Christ Will, you're going to let this be over before it even starts because it's too much work to express your feelings."

"Shut up," I mumbled, and took another drink. They weren't

wrong. I wasn't willing to ask Bea for what I needed, and that meant I would never get it. I put my drink down and pressed my hands to my eyes. I felt too warm, like I needed to get outside and away from the lights and Jun's piercing gaze.

"I can't ask a girl I barely know to move to Portland," I said.

"Can't you?"

I groaned. "I'm going to call her."

"Now, while you're drunk?"

I waved my hand vaguely at them. "It's New Year's. She's probably drunk too. Besides, I've only had the one." It was probably more like three, the way it was mixed, but I could handle it.

"You know what? If it was anyone else, I would tell them to wait," they said. "But you need a little bit of a shove to get anything done."

"I love you too," I grumbled.

I STEPPED ONTO the back porch and curled up in a very damp deck chair. Bea was still in my phone as "Betty Draper," and I hadn't had the heart to change it. I hit "Call" before I lost my nerve.

She didn't pick up.

I let the voice mail play out but didn't leave a message. There was really only one thing I could be calling about, and she would pick up or she wouldn't. I couldn't blame her for deciding that I wasn't worth the trouble. I sat in the cold chair, my sudden resolve and optimism gone. It was arrogant of me to think a phone call would fix this.

This was what all our conversations would be like, and I would have to accept that. A relationship in phone calls and stolen moments. I squeezed my eyes shut.

My phone vibrated in my hand.

I hit "Answer" immediately, and Bea's face popped up on Facetime. I swallowed.

"Hi," I said lamely.

She raised an eyebrow. "Filled with New Year's regret?"

"Well, yeah," I admitted. "I—I have a lot I wish I had said differently, and drunk at 11 p.m. on New Year's Eve seems like the right time to make up for it."

She hummed. "Drunk at 11 p.m. is not my preferred time for emotional conversations, actually."

"That's fair," I said quickly. "God, I'm sorry, I shouldn't—"

"Absolutely not. Tell me why you called me, and do it quickly before someone notices I snuck out the back." I opened my mouth, and she cut me off. "Actually, me first."

I nodded.

"You're a prick," she said. "You didn't have to act like I meant something if I didn't."

"You did mean something to me," I said. "You still do. I was…I was fighting with my mom, and I got overwhelmed and I shut down. That's not an excuse. You deserve better than that."

"No, I don't," she said quickly. Apparently, all of her resolve had been used up. "Parents are tough. I know that."

"You shouldn't have to suffer because I run away when I feel too many emotions, and you certainly shouldn't have to placate me through my fuck ups."

"What about forgiving you? Can I do that?"

I exhaled. "I would really like that."

"Then I forgive you. And I understand why dating me isn't very appealing—"

"That's not what the problem is at all."

"Fine," she said. "The logistics of dating me aren't very appealing."

"That's fair," I admitted. "It's not the drive, it's just…going back to that town stirs up a lot of bad memories for me. But the logistics of dating me aren't very appealing either. I get most of my self-worth from my job, and I have no sense of work-life balance. I'm obsessive about lists, and I don't like other people rearranging my silverware drawer, and I naturally wake up at 6 a.m. My apartment is the size of a shoebox, so when you visit, we'll have to share a twin bed." I took a deep breath. "But I want this to work. I want to sneak into town to visit you, and I want to show you around Portland, and I want to think that maybe, we're planning for a future together."

She giggled. "You really know how to romance a girl."

"I'm sorry," I said quickly. "I'm better at being practical than writing poetry, but I'll memorize sonnets if that's what you want."

"It's not important," she said. "If I wanted sonnets, I would date someone else." She looked down. "I don't know when I'll get out of town. There's too much to consider, and I'm no more impulsive than you are."

"We can make a plan," I said. "If you want to. If you want to stay…" I wanted to say that would be okay, but I knew I couldn't do long distance for an eternity. "If you want a small-town life, I'll still wish you all the happiness in the world."

"I'm not happy," she whispered, like a confession. "I didn't realize how unhappy I was, until you."

"You hide it well," I said. She was just like me, unwilling to face a fight. I couldn't blame her.

"It's different when I'm with you. You make me want to fight for something. You make me feel like maybe I have a future."

My throat was tight. "I know how you feel," I said.

She bit her lip. "Can I come visit you next week?"

"Yes," I said. "Yes, come visit as often as you want."

"I can use the soap money to pay for gas," she said. "People are still ordering."

"That's great," I said, and then, "Wiccans aren't supposed to do spells for personal gain, and I really want to see you."

"That seems like an overly strict interpretation of the rules," she said.

"Yeah," I agreed, "and fuck Wiccans."

Someone yelled in the background. She looked off screen for a minute, and then said, "I should probably go before people start getting weird."

I nodded. "I wish I could kiss you at midnight," I said.

"Next year," she promised. Then, she pressed her fingers to her lips and tapped the screen. I mimicked her action.

"Good night, Will," she said. "I'll see you soon."

About the Author:
Alec J. Marsh

ALEC LIVES IN the Pacific Northwest, where they write romantic adult fantasy and self-indulgent fanfiction. They make candles inspired by their favorite characters.

Links

Etsy: https://www.etsy.com/shop/speculativewicktion
Instagram: https://www.instagram.com/alecjmarsh/
Twitter: https://twitter.com/alecjmarsh

Titles by Alec J. Marsh

Heart's Scaffold
A Mutual Interest
Study Hall
To Drive the Hundred Miles

Anthologies including Alec J. Marsh

She Wears the Midnight Crown (author contributor)

About Duck Prints Press LLC

DUCK PRINTS PRESS LLC is an independent publisher based in New York State. Our founding vision is to help fanwork creators navigate the complex process of bringing their original works from first draft to print, culminating in publishing their work under our imprint. We are particularly dedicated to working with queer creators and publishing stories and artwork featuring characters from across the LGBTQIA+ spectrum.

Find us online at our website https://duckprintspress.com/ or on social media:

Bluesky: duckprintspress.bsky.social
Facebook: duckprintspress
Instagram: duckprintspress
TikTok: @duckprintspress
Tumblr: @duckprintspress

Goodreads:
https://www.goodreads.com/user/show/129902473-duck-prints-press-llc

Storygraph:
https://app.thestorygraph.com/profile/unforth

If you enjoyed this story, don't forget to leave us a review!

www.ingramcontent.com/pod-product-compliance
Lightning Source LLC
Chambersburg PA
CBHW070942250626
47159CB00009B/3356